# The Hidden Hollow

by Njord Kane

**The Hidden Hollow**
by Njord Kane



Library of Congress Control Number:  2017904974

Published on: September 1, 2017 by Spangenhelm Publishing

Interior Design and Cover by: Njord Kane

ISBN-13: 978-1943066230

ISBN-10: 194306623X

1. Fiction  2. Fantasy  3. Historical Fiction  4. Historical Fantasy

First Edition.

10 9 8 7 6 5 4 3 2 1

# Table of Contents

In a glaciated valley where green rocky slopes descended into the crisp blue waters of a long narrow Fjord, there stood the tall mossy thatched roof of a longhouse.

There was nothing particularly special about this long pitched roof from any of the other long pitched roofs scattered about on the sloped hills leading into the fjord. Except this particular long pitched roof belonged to the household of Bjord Argunson, the local blacksmith.

Bjord's longhouse was easy to pick out because of the black smoke that often bellowed out from the fires of his forge burning inside.  One didn't suffer the cold of winter inside the house of a blacksmith...

# Chapter 1

Rowan woke up startled late in the night. He dreamt that he was submerged in the cold waters of the fjord while someone stood on his chest and held him underwater. It felt like he was drowning in his sleep.

Although he was now awake, it still felt like something heavy was pressing down on his chest. He slowly opened his eyes and was surprised at what he saw.

There was a rather large house cat sitting on his chest.

It just sat there on his chest looking down at him with its yellow eyes that seemed to glow in the darkness.  Eyes that seemed to be looking directly into his very soul.  It was the largest cat that he'd ever seen and it was heavy.  It wasn't a mountain lion or anything like that.  It was just a simple orange house cat, but it was the biggest one he'd ever seen.

Rowan wasn't sure if he was still half asleep and still dreaming, but the cat seemed to be getting heavier and heavier as it sat on his chest. It wasn't moving, it just sat on his chest staring down at him.

The cat felt like it weighed as much as a large man.

Its unusual weight had Rowan pinned down underneath it. He wasn't able to move and it was making it harder and harder for him to breathe.

Rowan tried to get the cat off of him but it simply wouldn't budge and ignored his attempts.  It was definitely getting heavier and heavier. The cat was now making it nearly impossible for him to breathe. It was also starting to crush his chest under its growing impossible weight.  Rowan tried to roll to his side to knock the cat off, but was unable to move.

He was now starting to suffocate under its weight. He tried to call out but couldn't.  He needed to wake someone up and get help.  If he didn't get the cat off him it was going to kill him.

He was starting to panic. Rowan kicked up his legs in a desperate attempt to get the cat off of him, but failed.

The cat slowly leaned its head down closer towards Rowan's face and loudly hissed the most horrible and eerie hiss that he'd ever heard in his life.

It leapt off his chest and left him choking and gasping for air.

The cat took a few steps back before it turned around and let out a horrendous screech that woke the entire household out of their slumbers.  It then ran screeching towards the barn at the other end of the house where the family's livestock was kept.

In the barn there were three cows and six sheep; not to mention one missing temperamental goat, which the blacksmith's family had appropriately named, "Grumpy."

Grumpy usually wasn't in the barn because he didn't like being with the rest of the livestock. He never stayed in his pen because felt he was much too important to be considered with the cows and sheep. Most mornings, members of the household would wake up to see Grumpy standing over them chewing on whatever mischief he'd gotten his chompers into this time. Whenever anyone got up to put him back into his pen, he'd protest with a loud bleat and have to be dragged back into his pen as he resisted the entire way.

The cat charged into the barn howling its ghastly screech, which in turn, caused the sheep to panic and break out of their pens.  They near trampled over each other as they quickly scurried out through the door in a frenzied attempt to get away from the maniacal cat.

The cows managed to snap their tethers and quick footed their way to the blacksmithing area on the other end of the longhouse.  This was where Bjord Argunson worked his trade.

There was a large forge and an anvil stone which was set deep into the ground. The anvil stone was much too large to have been brought into the house when it was built.  The blacksmith's house had been built over the massive anvil stone to accompany the smith's needs.

It was also where the goat was perched, having already made its usual rebellious nightly escape before this commotion even started.

The panic stricken sheep that ran outside screaming into the darkness were now out of sight with the ghoulish cat in hot pursuit behind them howling demoniacally.

Everyone in the longhouse quickly rose out of their beds wide eyed and in a panicked frenzy. Nobody knew what was going on.  It was the most frightening and unnerving sound any of them had ever heard.

Bjord sprang from his bed and quickly ran over to grab a torch.  He lit it from the central fire pit and used it to look around the longhouse.  Seeing no threat, but terrified animals and his knocked over work bench, he rushed outside to investigate. The screaming sheep could still be heard in the darkness as they fled from the cat.

Everyone else, including Rowan, rushed outside behind him to see what was happening.  Sven grabbed a torch and lit it from the hearth fire and also an ax to arm himself. The fear in his eyes was obvious. He wasn't about to step outside unarmed.

The sheep were gone. They could still be heard off in the distance madly running up the hill in the darkness. The unnatural howls of the cat chasing behind them could also be heard. It was obviously trying to run them to their deaths.

"What just happened," asked Bjord as he walked back towards the longhouse holding the torch up high in the air as he looked around.

"A feral cat I think," said Rowan half afraid to answer and a bit unsure himself of what had just happened.

"A feral cat," said Bjord. "Are you kidding me?"

Rowan nodded while shielding his eyes from the torch's light as Bjord stood in front of him.

"I woke up and there was a cat sitting on my chest."

Bjord cocked his head to the side and gave Rowan an odd look.

"A cat was sitting on your chest?"

"Yes, it was sitting on my chest and then it started getting heavier," Rowan said. "I wasn't sure if I was just dreaming until it started to take away my breath."

"It tried to take away your breath?"

"Yes," said Rowan, "it kept getting heavier and heavier as it sat on my chest. It felt like it was trying to crush me. Then when I tried to get it off me, it got even bigger and heavier until I couldn't move or breathe at all."

Bjord wasn't believing any of Rowan's story and was starting to get angry at this point.

"I can't believe I am listening to this nonsense," he said.

"I managed to roll to my side a little and that was when it hissed," Rowan said, "it then jumped off me and ran after the sheep in the barn."

Sven just stood there bewildered with his torch held up high trying to peer into the darkness towards the distant sounds.

"A cat?"

"That was no cat," said Helga, "that was a draug."

Grandmother Helga had been standing in the doorway behind everyone else, still wrapped tightly in her blanket.

"A draug? What, pray tell, is a draug if I dare ask," Bjord said mockingly.

"Yes, a draug," she said scornfully, not liking Bjord's mocking tone. "It's a person that has risen from the dead, cursed to walk among us again by its own obsessions or hatred."

"Oh yes, I remember my grandfather telling me tall stories about dead walkers," said Bjord. "But he also spoke of many other unseen beings in the forests and mountains from the myths of old."

Bjord started to laugh.

"He also talked about such things as trolls and elves too."

"And you should heed his warning about such creatures," she said waving her finger at him.

"Nobody's ever seen such a thing and I don't mean any disrespect, but Grandfather also used to run outside naked flapping his arms squeaking like a bird too," Bjord said with a laugh.  He was referring to when his grandfather began to become a bit 'touched' in the head in his final years.

Helga just looked at him with contempt in her eyes and then threw her arms up in the air as she turned around and went back inside the longhouse.

"It will try to run the sheep to their deaths. That's what the ancient legends say they do. It's fortunate that the cows didn't run with them, otherwise they'd be lost too," she added as she disappeared inside.

"I'm not going to lose my sheep to a cursed feral cat," said Bjord angrily. "Draugs, or whatever you call them, are nothing but a superstition."

He turned back towards Rowan and said, "fetch my ax and grab some torches. We're going to get those sheep back."

Without answering Rowan immediately ran inside to grab the things his master demanded.

Bjord then turned towards his stepson Sven.

"Boy! Grab some rope to tether the sheep so we can bring them back."

Sven ran inside the longhouse to gather some rope. Rowan grabbed Bjord's battle ax that was hung on the wall near the blacksmith's favorite place to sit.

He briefly looked at Bjord's shield hanging next to it but decided not to grab it. He picked up an armful of unlit torches and then ran back outside with his bundle.  He delivered the ax to Bjord.

Rowan was busy binding the torches together with some twine so he could sling them across his back when Sven came back outside with the rope.

They shared a brief look when he walked by and tossed it on the ground in front of Rowan.

Rowan knew how lazy Sven could be and without changing beat, picked up the rope and slung it over his shoulder.

Still holding his torch up, Bjord walked over to the edge of the treeline where the sheep had ran. He stood there for a moment staring into the darkness, contemplating whether or not to try to find them in the dark or not.

Sven and Rowan quickly joined him and quietly stood waiting behind him.

Bjord held the torch in the air and kept looking into the darkness for a few moments until he finally lowered his shoulders and turned towards them with a defeated look on his face.

"We're not going to find them in the dark. We will have wait until morning when we have sunlight. We will have to track them down then."

He looked at Sven, who was standing there wide-eyed and speechless with a torch in one hand and an ax in the other.  Rowan peered into the forest's darkness with a worried look on his face. He knew nobody believed him, but that was no ordinary house cat.

"Let's get some sleep and go after them in the morning," Bjord said as he started walking back towards the longhouse.

Sven and Rowan did not dawdle and quickly followed behind him, periodically casting a worried look over their shoulder towards the forest as they went.

# Chapter 2

The morning came fast with little sleep for the blacksmith's still shaken household. The events just hours ago had left everyone sleeping with one eye opened and their ears perked for even the slightest sound.

Nobody was granted a restful sleep.

Rowan couldn't find it within himself to sleep lying on his back for fear of the cat coming back and trying to seat itself on his chest again.

Perhaps this time the cat would be successful and end him before he'd be able to wake up in time. This time he slept, or rather attempted to sleep, he stayed on his side to prevent anything from resting on his chest.

Rowan was a thrall who'd been in the blacksmith's household since he was a small lad. He was sold to the blacksmith by a trader who'd found him in the burnt rubble of his family's longhouse in another land across the sea.

Rowan was too small to remember who the invaders were that attacked and destroyed his village, but he knew the raiders had meant for there to be no survivors.

The trader that found him came the morning after the invaders had left to scavenge through the ruins. While rummaging, he discovered Rowan hiding under a table in the ruins of his charred home and took him aboard his ship.

The man sold him to the blacksmith for less than the price of a calf

After the blacksmith put an iron ring around Rowan's neck and cropped his hair short, he was immediately put to work chopping wood and tending to the livestock.

He'd been in the blacksmith's household for twelve winters now.

When the light shined through the doorway and announced daybreak had come, Rowan was relieved. He was tired, but he was glad to have made it through the rest of the night.

He knew he'd better not dawdle in his daily tasks, so he got up and went to the barn area to milk the cows. Being mindful not to disturb anyone, he fetched the milking bucket and noticed that the goat was still at the other end of the house standing on the anvil. It just stood there looking back at him.

Obliviously Grumpy didn't get any sleep either and had kept a vigilance throughout the rest of the night perched up on the anvil stone.

It made Rowan smile.

*"Don't worry goat, I didn't get any sleep either."*

Rowan slowly moved around in the barn and positioned himself next to one of the cow.  He was being extra ginger with her because he figured that she may still be a bit skittish from last night.  Calmly he reassured her until he felt she was calm enough to began milking.  He reached down to position the bucket and noticed something inside it.

There was something wrapped in a piece of cloth. Rowan reached down in the bucket and picked it up. It was a piece of Helga's scarf.  He unwrapped it and found one of her honey biscuits.

Rowan smiled, knowing that she'd left that intentionally for him to find.

He quickly wrapped it back up and stuffed it in his shirt.

The milking had to be done first thing in the

morning.  Gwenda, Bjord's wife, wanted to make as much cheese as possible before the cows started to slow their milk at the end of the season. The milk would have to be set out to curd.

He began steadily milking the cow.

Suddenly a voice came from behind Rowan.

"Forget the milking today."

It was Bjord.

He startled both Rowan and the cow who mooed in protest while taking a step sideways.

"Thelsa will finish doing it," Bjord said referring to his young daughter who was just a year or so younger than Rowan.

Rowan looked up at Bjord and nodded.  He hung the milking bucket up on a hook so the cows wouldn't kick it over and followed Bjord out of the barn.

"Thelsa," said Bjord loud enough to stir everyone else in the house out of their peaceful slumber. "Thelsa, get up! Get up and finish the milking!"

Thelsa was still dazed in the drink of sleep and tried rubbing the sleep from her eyes while she got out of bed.

"That's the thrall's job..."

"Do what I tell you lazy girl," said Bjord, cutting her off before she could finish protesting.

He turned back towards Rowan and said, "go gather some rope, enough to tie all of the sheep so we can bring them back."

Rowan quickly scampered off to gather rope as Bjord walked by Sven's bed and kicked him on the bottom of his feet.

"Get up boy, it's time to fetch those sheep," Bjord said. "Make sure you grab your bow."

Bjord began gathered supplies himself and stuffed them into a leather shoulder bag while Sven put his boots on.

Gwenda got up and added some wood to the cooking fire and began stoking it up.

"Do you want me to cook you anything before you go," Gwenda asked.

"No, I'll just grab some dried meat to take with us. I don't think we'll be gone very long."

Bjord walked over by Gwenda and grabbed some of the dried meat that was hanging on a hook next to her. He cut off several chunks off and stuffed them into his shoulder pack.

"Those sheep couldn't have ran off very far," he said before embracing his wife and then turning to head out the door.

"Come on boys, I want to get this over with. We have lots to do when we get back. There's really no time to be messing around looking for skittish sheep that are afraid of their own shadows."

The three of them, Bjord, Sven, and Rowan, left the longhouse and set out in the direction the sheep had ran last night. They entered the forest following the trail the sheep left behind as they tore across the field and into the woods.

They were heading directly up the hillside.

Rowan didn't like the idea of going into the forest up the hillside. He had a bad feeling about it. The sheep were always too skittish to even get close to the wood line and enter the forest. It was just something they'd never do, especially towards the hillside.  They had to of been really scared to purposely run in that direction. They always steered well away from the woods when they grazed. It was odd that they'd intentionally run into the woods and not steer away, even if something was chasing them.

Rowan shook these thoughts off. Such worrying thoughts were meaningless. There wasn't anything that happened last night that made any sense. So why should the sheep running in the woods make any sense.

After awhile the trail began to lead into the thicker trees and brush of the forest that led up the mountainside. This area was seldom, if at all, ever ventured into by anyone from the village.

Superstitious or not, nobody wanted to venture too far into the wilderness and never be heard from again.

Bjord noticed something ahead in the bushes and stopped dead in his tracks. He reached over and caught Sven by the shoulder who'd walked past him not paying any attention.

"Look," he said. "There's something in that bush."

Sven looked around for a moment, but didn't see anything at first, then gasped as soon as he noticed it.

Rowan stood behind them and looked around nervously.

"Go see what it is," Bjord said while nudging Sven forward.

Sven gulped and looked back at his father with a horrified look on his face, but before he could say anything, Bjord stepped past him to go look himself.

"Never mind boy."

Rowan and Sven cautiously followed behind Bjord to get a better look at what was in the bush.

It was one of the sheep.

"That's one of them," Sven said as he looked over his stepfather's shoulder. "It's been freshly shorn and it's wearing one of our collars. That's one of ours."

All the livestock belonging to the blacksmith's household wore a leather collar that had a single iron ring hanging from it inscribed with the word, 'Bjord' to mark his ownership of them.

Even Rowan's neck collar was inscribed similarly with the word, 'Bjord.' The only real difference was the livestock's collars were made from leather, while Rowan's collar was made from iron.

Bjord bent down to get a closer look at it.

"You could tell it ran itself to death, its eyes are still wide open from fear," he said.

Rowan said nothing and just stood there looking around. This place made him feel very uneasy. Something about these woods just wasn't right and he knew it. He didn't know why, but he knew they shouldn't be there.

He also felt that the sheep weren't worth whatever awaited them in the hills.

Bjord looked up towards where the trail continued and tried to determine what to do next when Sven interrupted him.

"I'm hungry, can we stop and eat," Sven asked.

Bjord turned around and looked at Sven for a moment. He was just about to say something, but then dropped his shoulders and softened up.

"Yes, we should rest a moment and grab a bite to eat. There is no sense continuing on with an empty stomach."

Bjord removed his shoulder bag and sat down on the ground with his back to a tree. Sven and Rowan sat down next to him as he reached into his bag and pulled out a thick slice of meat. It was a slice from a haunch of smoked boar that he packed before they left.

He tore the chunk of meat into two halves and handed the smaller one to Sven while keeping the larger portion for himself.

Rowan wasn't given anything to eat and just sat there awkwardly looking off into the woods while waiting for them to finish.  He was hungry and remembered the sweet bread that Helga had left for him, but knew if he took it out that Sven would just take it from him and eat it in front of him.

After Bjord was satisfied with having eaten and resting enough, he put the remainder of his chunk of meat in his bag and stood up, wiping his hands on his pants and dusting off his woolen trousers.

Rowan taking the hint, stood up as well and adjusted the rope he was carrying over his shoulder.

Bjord looked down at Sven, who was still gnawing on his meat and ignoring everyone.

"Come on boy, you can eat that as we go. We haven't got all day."

Without waiting for him to get up, Bjord turned and began walking through the woods continuing to follow the trail the remaining sheep had made. Rowan followed behind him, taking a final look at the dead sheep in the bush.

Sven suddenly noticing that he was alone, quickly got up and followed.  He took a few more bites off his chunk of meat before tossing it into the bushes.

Rowan heard him throw it and it skitter through the bushes as his stomach grumbled slightly at the thought of it.  He didn't give Sven the satisfaction by looking. He was quite used to this kind of treatment, besides, he still had a sweet bread tucked in his shirt. A hunk of Helga's honey biscuits which were irresistible to Sven.

He'd enjoy that by himself later.

As a thrall, he wasn't mistreated or even abused. He knew he was fortunate to be owned by the blacksmith because he'd seen how other thralls were treated by other owners. Many of them were regularly abused and quite often beaten. Rowan had never been beaten or harshly mistreated. He was often secretly given treats such as this by Helga.

Bjord motioned forward and said, "come on, we've got to find the others."

They continued to follow the trail left behind by the running sheep. Sven and Rowan followed behind Bjord while he tracked their way up the mountain. Their route was gradually starting to incline steeper as they went further and further into the forest.

They were beginning to become winded after a while and Bjord decided to stop and rest.  He sat on a large rock while the other two sat down on the ground near him.

It was then that Rowan noticed that something just wasn't right around them.

The forest was just simply too quiet.

The usual sounds of wildlife and birds were missing. There was an unsettling stillness in the forest. The only thing that could be heard were the occasional sounds of leaves rustling when the wind blew, but that was all.

It was too quiet.

"Do you hear that," Rowan asked.

Bjord straightened up and listened for a minute.

"Hear what," he said. "I don't hear anything."

"I don't hear anything either," Sven said.

"Exactly," Rowan said. "There aren't any sounds out there. Not even the birds are chirping."

They quietly listened for a moment. Sven began to look openly worried, but Bjord shrugged it off as he stood up and grabbed his pack.

"Come on, we've got to find those sheep."

They continued up following the trail until they came upon another dead sheep lying on the ground halfway in a bush. It was like the first one, in that you could tell it ran itself to death in total fear.

Sven shuddered at the sight of it.

"Rowan," Bjord said, "pull that sheep out of the bushes. I want to be able to find it on our way back. I am sure we can salvage the hide and some of the meat from it."

Rowan did as he was told and pulled the sheep out of the bush where it had fallen.

Sven stood back and watched, offering absolutely no assistance. Not that Rowan expected any help. He was used to Sven idly watching him. It just amused him how much Sven seemed to be afraid to touch it.

After Rowan had the sheep pulled away from the bush, Bjord turned and continued walking up the hillside. There was still a visible track and he meant to follow it until he found all of his sheep.

"Keep moving," he said, "there's still four sheep that may still be alive. That is, if the wolves don't find them before we do."

As they proceeded further up the hillside, ever determined, the trees and brush began to get even thicker. Even though it was only midday, the foliage became denser and was starting to make it darker and darker around them.

Pushing their way forward, they were suddenly overwhelmed by the most horrendous smell of rotten decay.

It seemed to linger thick in the air and cling to everything like a thick invisible fog. It permeated the air as if it had been there for quite awhile.

The strong stench made Sven gag.

"What's that smell," he said. "It's awful!"

"Something dead nearby," said Bjord. "Keep going, it'll pass."

Bjord used the sleeve of his shirt to cover his mouth and nose from the odor as he marched forward following the trail left behind by the sheep.

Rowan had never smelled anything like it before. He'd once came across a rotting boar carcass in the forest when he was gathering wood. The boar was discolored, bloated, and very putrid. It was definitely dead and it has definitely been there for a while. It laid in a patch of sunlight that beamed in through a clearing of the trees. It was so putrid, not even the flies wanted it.

The smell in the air now was similar, but way worse than the stench of the boar he found.  It made Rowan's stomach churn in a most unpleasant way. He tried using his sleeve to cover the smell, but it didn't help.

It didn't take long for all three of them to start turning green from the smell.

They stopped in their tracks and were all trying to cover their noses and mouths as best as they could.

"Well,.."

*[Bjord abruptly stopped talking to gag]*

"Well, we've indeed found something unpleasant lurking about here."

"Something's definitely dead near here and I don't think it's any of the sheep," Sven said.

"I agree," Bjord said. "They haven't been dead long enough to rot and smell like that. Plus the other two sheep we found didn't smell like that."

Sven and Rowan both nodded in agreement, not wanting to speak and uncover their mouths any more than they had to.

"Whatever it is," Bjord said, "it's been dead for awhile. I don't know what would make such a stench, but I don't think I want to find out."

The notion made both Sven and Rowan turn pale as their hearts fearfully sank. They've all heard the stories about the things that supposedly lived in the forest and in the mountains. Places said to be forbidden to men where both unseen folk and beings from the legends were said to inhabit.

In the brush ahead they could clearly see where the remaining sheep had ran. They ran right through breaking branches and everything else in their way. It was obvious that they were desperate to escape whatever was chasing them.

The entire trail had been this way. It didn't take any real tracking skills to follow the panicking sheep's path taken.

They stopped following the trail when it ended at some dense bushes. Bjord scratched the back of his head and knelt down to examine the broken branches on the bushes.

"They must have been cornered and then they ran right through the bush," he said.

He bent down and plucked a piece of wool from a branch and stood back up.

"Yes, I do believe that is what happened. Here's a piece of wool from one of them. They tore through those bushes and made their own path."

Sven and Rowan just looked at each other, not sure what to think about the whole ordeal.

After a moment of kneeling back down and trying to look through the hole in the bushes, Bjord stood up and motioned to Rowan while pointing at the hole.

"Crawl though there and see if you can tell where they went."

Rowan silently gulped and nodded.

He wasn't sure what lay beyond those bushes and whether or not he wanted to meet it face to face while crawling on his hands and knees through the bushes.

He removed the rope he was carrying over his shoulder and set it down on the ground.  Rowan got down on his hands and knees and carefully began crawling through the hole in the bushes. He could see light on the other side.

It looked like it was only a few paces from where the sheep had gone in and then busted out through the other side.

Rowan crawled through hole. It was only as high as he was on his hands and knees and was barely wide enough for his body to pass easily. He continued to crawl through the bush to the other side.

When he came out through the other side, Rowan got quite the startle when he almost fell to his death.

Abruptly on the other side of the thick bushes which the sheep had ran though was a steep cliff.

It was a very steep cliff that dropped for a very long way.

Rowan carefully backed up trying not to fall off over the side.  He turned and called back,"there's a cliff at the other end of these bushes!"

"What," asked Bjord. "What do you see?"

'There's a steep cliff that goes down the mountainside," said Rowan.

Bjord drew his brows together and wrinkled his forehead, giving Sven a puzzled look.

"Do you see any of the sheep?"

Rowan edged closer to the side and looked over.

All he could see was a abrupt decline that fell several ways down into the rocks below. He gasped and safely scooted himself back again. He turned and yelled back.

"I don't see them," he said. "It falls straight down into rocks. There is no sign of them down there."

Bjord looked down and sighed. After mumbling something under his breath about 'thralls,' he looked back up at Sven.

"Go in there and look," he said. "Tell me if you can see where the sheep went."

Sven did not want to go in there.

Regardless of his daydreaming about becoming a legendary hero, he wasn't exactly 'hero' material. But before he could make any kind of protest, Bjord frowned at him and motioned towards the hole torn in the bush.

"Go now boy!"

Sven nodded and removed his bow and leather weaved quiver, setting them down on top of where Rowan had set the rope.

Reluctantly he knelt down to crawl through the hole and paused a second to look through it.  He could see Rowan at the other end.

30

"Go on boy," Bjord said, "nothing's going to get you."

Sven nodded and looked back at his quiver real quick to make sure that he set it down so that none of the arrows would fall out and noticed that he'd grabbed the wrong quiver.

In his haste this morning, he grabbed the quiver contained fishing arrows. They had bone tips with small barbs in them. They were useless for anything else besides fishing because they shattered when they hit against anything other than a fish in the water.

They were not the sharp iron tipped arrows for hunting he needed in case they came across some wolves or something and needed to defend themselves.

He hoped his stepfather didn't notice his bumble because he knew he'd never hear the end of it. Thankfully, he seriously doubted that he'd even need to use his bow. He just didn't want to catch hell for grabbing the wrong quiver of arrows.

Bjord was beginning to grow openly annoyed at Sven's hesitation and kicked him on the rump with the side of his foot, shoving him forward.

"Get in there boy," he said, "stop being a damned coward."

Sven crawled through the passage to the other end where Rowan was knelt down patiently waiting. He tore a hole in his trousers while he was crawling and cursed at Rowan for it.

"You're going to be the one sewing these back together," he said as he scooted next to Rowan.

Sven carefully looked over the edge to see what was there. Rowan grabbed him on the shoulder and steadied him when he saw him flinch near the edge.

"Be careful," he said.

He just shot Rowan a dirty look and said, "don't worry thrall, I've got this. Don't touch me."

Sven hesitantly looked further over the side and carefully scanned the area below in disbelief. All he could see was a sudden steep drop to the rocks down below.  He looked at Rowan with a baffled look of disbelief on his face.

Rowan nodded in agreement and looked over the side again himself.

Sven slowly backed away from the ledge and called back to Bjord.

"It's true," he said, "there's a sudden drop over a cliff at the end of the passage. It's a long drop and there are rocks below. Nothing could survive that kind of a fall."

"Do you see any sign of the sheep," Bjord asked.

"I don't see any sign of the sheep," Sven said. "It's like they just disappeared. I can't say for sure, but I don't see any of their bodies anywhere down there."

Puzzled, Bjord angrily cursed under his breath.

"Go ahead and come back through," he told them. "Make sure you look one last time to make sure there's no sign of them. They had to go somewhere. Sheep just don't disappear in thin air."

"We're coming back out," Sven called back.

He didn't need to be told twice to get out of there. He didn't want to crawl through that hole in the first place, and he absolutely did not like being next to that cliff with its sudden drop to a guaranteed death.

Sven crawled back out through the hole with Rowan following closely behind.

When Sven got through, he quickly stood up and began brushing the dirt off from his hands and knees before he gathered up his bow and quiver.

Rowan crawled out and had to step around Sven who was still blocking the exit.  He picked the rope up from the ground and slung it back over his shoulder.

The air was still thick with a putrid smell of something dead and rotten. Sven covered his nose and mouth with the inside of his arm and tried not to gag from it.  When they crawled through the hole, the air on the other side was much clearer and didn't reek.  It was only when they crawled back that the smell hit them again.

"What is that smell," said Sven to nobody in particular.

Bjord said, "I don't know, but it can't be from the sheep. Even if they'd been dead for a long time, they wouldn't leave behind a stench such as that. This smell is from something that has been rotting for a very long time. It is not natural."

"There was no real proof that the sheep ran over the cliff," Bjord said. "Although wolves or something could have carried them off, I don't think so. They also could have seen the cliff and turned around."

He wasn't going to be satisfied unless he'd given the area a proper look.  He wasn't going to give up losing his livestock so easily.

"Let's go further up the hill and see what we can find out," he said. "Maybe the sheep ran up there. The brush is very thick, but we can still get through this way."

He indicted which direction they were going by pointing towards a less dense area and started walking towards it.

Bjord led the way as they made their way through the thicket up the hill. He used his ax to chop some of branches and limbs out of the way to clear their passage.

The smell of decay was getting even more intense as they progressed. Sven stopped once when his stomach couldn't handle it anymore and retched out his earlier meal.

Rowan secretly got some satisfaction from watching him. Sven hadn't the common compassion to share his meat and had tossed the remainder in the woods. Now he was paying for it.

Having an empty stomach now paid off for Rowan, even though he wasn't sure for how much longer.

When they finally got through and came out of the thick brush to a clearing on the other side, Sven dropped to his knees and started gagging again. On the other side, there was a rocky clearing with very little brush on it.  In the middle of the clearing was a mound of piled stones and dirt.  The mound was completely clear of any brush or grass.

It seemed barren as if nothing would grow on it.

The putrid smell in the air was now worse than it ever had been before. It smelled as if there were rotten corpses all over the place, even though there was nothing but the barren mound of stone and soil.

"What is this place," asked Sven as he gasped from the stench in the air.

"I don't know," said Bjord, "it appears to be a burial mound."

"A burial mound?"

Sven was beside himself in near disbelief.

"Are you sure?"

"Yes, I know a burial mound when I see one," said Bjord, "but what I don't get is why it's way up here hidden in the forest on the mountain and why the dirt looks fresh. It looks like it was just made."

Rowan just stood behind them, covering his nose and mouth, trying to not get sick from the stench that lingered in the air.

Bjord walked toward the mound to get a closer look at it while the other two slowly moved behind him keeping their distance.

"I don't understand why it smells so bad,' said Bjord as he looked at the mound closely with his eyes visibly starting to water from the offensive smell in the air.

"What do you mean," asked Sven.

"Well for one," said Bjord, "whatever is buried

here shouldn't be smelling like this because it's buried and there's nothing exposed here to make the smell."

Bjord bent down on one knee to get an closer look at the soil on the mound and brushed some of it to the side.

"Yes," he said, "the soil appears to be fairly fresh. But look, there's river stones with moss on it like it's been here for years. But why river stones?"

"So what," said Sven, "lots of people use river stones for burial mounds."

"Yeah, but not way up here on the mountain side. They would have had to carry those stones all the way up here. Why not just use the rock and stone that was already up here?"

"Look," said Sven, "there's a mist here."

Everyone looked around and noticed that a heavy mist was beginning to form around them. It was coming from out of the mound itself.

Sven and Rowan exchanged a worried look.

"This isn't right," Sven said.

"Mists don't just form out of nowhere and they don't form that fast either. Something isn't right about this," he said as he started backing up.

Bjord stood up and looked around as he backed away. The mist had become dense all around them.

Just as he was about to say something, they all noticed a dark figure standing in front of them on top of the burial mound.

It had just sort of 'appeared' there in the mist.

The smell of death in the air was stronger than it had ever been before.

"What is that," asked Sven as he gagged from the stench that was thick in the air.

"Who's there?" Bjord demanded of the large figure standing in the mist.

Bjord lifted his battle ax and gripped the handle tightly with both hands. He glanced at Sven and said, "get an arrow ready boy."

The mist was starting to fade away and they were able to get a better look at the figure standing in front of them.  None of them were prepared for what they saw.

It stood there twice as tall as a man and bloated twice as wide. Its rotting head was pink and purplish blue with large dead white eyes that glared through swollen eyelids.

The smell of decay that came from it was so strong that it sickened everyone to a point of actually making them want to drop to their knees and start gagging.  It made them want to wretch, but fear from the very sight of this thing prevented any action from any of them but to gaze at it in horror.

It was the 'draug' that Grandmother Helga had warned them about.

The ghastly thing stood there for a moment looking at them menacingly before it let out a piercing scream and leapt forward at Bjord.

It pounced right on top of Bjord before he could react.

He was still in shock from seeing this creature. Even though he had his ax at the ready, it was useless in his hands and he fell to the ground with the creature on top of him.

Bjord's face was turning red as he struggled under the weight of the beast. It had him pinned down with its knee was on his arm, preventing him from raising his ax.

He was pinned down, helpless and completely unable to defend himself. That was when the ghastly thing brought its huge fist down upon him and smashed him in the chest.

The powerful hit made Bjord gasp painfully for air before spitting out some blood.

Both Sven and Rowan stood frozen for a moment with their mouths agape looking on in shock before they were able to react.

Sven, seeing that it was killing his stepfather, grabbed his bow and retrieved one of the bone tipped fishing arrows. He nocked the arrow, drew back and released it into the side of the creature.

The beast was so large that it was nearly impossible to miss and the arrow struck its target, piercing deeply into its rotting flesh.

The arrow strike didn't even phase it and the creature struck Bjord again with its massive fist while letting out a horrifying roar.

Sven released another arrow and pierced it deeply again.  The creature didn't even flinch.  It was as if the thing didn't even notice the arrows that Sven was firing into it.

Rowan was now able to move from the initial shock and took the small ax from his belt and hurdled it at the beast. He was hoping to sink the ax blade deep into the monster's skull.

Unfortunately the ax simply tumbled through the air and just swished pass the creature's head. He missed completely and the ax fell behind the mound.

Lost forever in the grass and brush.

Rowan just stared in disbelief in the general location where the ax had fell.  He didn't know what made him think he could have actually hit the creature with it. He'd never thrown an ax before in his life. He'd seen one of the men from the village throw one into a tree truck and was impressed by it. He never considered considered the fact that such a skill would actually take practice.

Now he was disarmed because of his foolish act.

Sven paid no attention to what Rowan was doing and sunk another arrow into the beast. Regardless of yet another arrow finding its mark and sinking deeply, the beast continued to ignore the arrows as if they weren't even there.

The draug was in a fury.  It continued to strike ferociously at Bjord who was no longer moving and didn't appear to even be alive anymore.

Rowan now disarmed and knowing he had to do something, mustered the courage to get closer and try to fetch the large battle ax that Bjord had dropped when the creature leapt on him.

Rowan gathered up his courage and took a running leap towards the ax. He tried to keep out of the creature's reach and slid past, trying to grab the ax as he went by.  Rowan seized the ax and tumbled clumsily forward and landed on his face flat on the ground.

He quickly got back up to his feet and picked up the ax with both hands.

Bjord's ax was a large solid ax meant to bash through shields.

Rowan gripped it tightly and raised it above his head and then brought it down upon the beast with all his might.

He sunk the ax deeply into the creature's back.

In contrast to the arrows embedded in its flesh that the creature had been ignoring, it did not ignore the ax penetrating it.

It roared violently in pain as it turned around and swatted Rowan with the back of its fist.

The blow knocked Rowan back several feet and tumble hard to the ground.

Rowan had never been hit that hard in his life. His head spun and the wind had been knocked out of him. He struggled to get up to his knees while he gasped for air.

The creature was violently turning about trying to grab and pull out the ax that was stuck in its back.

Sven continued firing his remaining arrows into the draug with no affect. The beast was completely unconcerned with the arrows and appeared to still be ignoring them.

The ax embedded into its back definitely had its full attention as it continued to struggle trying to reach back and pull it out.

The creature turned its back towards Rowan and he could see that the ax was actually burning the creature's decaying flesh.

The flesh around the ax head was sizzling and starting to bubble.  He saw smoke coming out from around the wound.

Sven fired his last arrow into the howling beast and then threw his bow down on the ground. He grabbed the ax that hanging from his belt and armed himself with it.

The beast was still reeling in pain and trying to free the ax from its back.

Sven saw that Rowan was disarmed and struggling to get backup to his feet.

He knew what he had to do.

Sven mustered all the courage he could and charged at the creature while it flailed about trying to get the ax out.  He swung his ax and sliced it on the arm.

The creature released an ear piecing roar and

turned to face Sven as he swung his ax again. This time he only nicked it on the forearm.

This only angered the creature even more.

In a raging fury, it reached over and grabbed Sven by the head with its massive hands and flung him high in the air.

He landed in the brush on the other side of the mound near the cliff and nearly tumbled over the side.

Sven struggled to get up, but wasn't able and collapsed.

Blinding pain radiated throughout his body and when he tried to call out for help, he was only able to spit out blood and slump to the ground.

The draug clinched its fists and angrily roared at Sven's motionless body on the ground.

Rowan was able to get to his feet and quickly looked around for a weapon.  Any kind of weapon. A rock. Stick. Anything that he could use as a weapon.

The creature was infuriated.  It stomped over to where Sven was laying on the ground and roared at his unconscious body.

Reaching down and grabbing Sven by the chest and leg, it picked him up and lifted him up above its head.  The beast then let out a ferocious roar and threw Sven's broken body over the side of the cliff.

Sven couldn't even scream.

Rowan was unarmed and there was nothing he could do. He could see that the ax he embedded into the back of the creature was still burning it. After it hurled Sven over the cliff, it continued struggling to reach the ax and pull it out from its back.

Rowan knew he wouldn't be able to take the creature out. He had managed to wound it, but that was pure luck and he no longer had a weapon anyways.

He took one last look at Bjord's lifeless broken body on the ground and turned towards the hole in the brush where they originally had came through and ran for his life.

He charged through the partially cut branches as if they weren't even there. Pushing through the branches in a desperate fury to escape the deadly wrath of the angered beast.

As he was passing through the thickest part of the brush he heard the draug roaring behind him.

It had seen him flee and gave chase.

Just as Rowan reached the other side, he heard the beast howl and start charging through the brush after him.

Rowan looked around in every direction trying to decide what to do. If he ran down the path they came up, the beast would surely catch up to him and run him down.

He looked through the hole in the bushes where the sheep had ran over the side of the cliff and decided to crawl through it in an attempt to hide from the creature.

Rowan quickly scurried through the hole and reached the other side near the cliff. He heard it growl on the other side of the bushes where he had just been seconds ago.

The creature wasn't fooled and didn't continued down the pass as Rowan had hoped it would.

It knew that he'd gone through the bush to hide.

Rowan was trapped and had to do something quick.  But he was cornered at the edge of a steep cliff with no where to go.

He realized that he still had the rope slung over his shoulders and removed it.  He took hold of one end and looked for something to tie it to.  He was going to try to lower himself down the side of the cliff and escape the creature.

Rowan searched for something sturdy to tie the

rope and decided on the base of a bush that appeared to be deeply rooted.

The creature began to force its way through the hole towards him.

Rowan's hands were shaking as he tied the knot and secured it to the base of the bush stump. He quickly tossed the other end down the side of the cliff and glimpsed over. The rope wasn't long enough and didn't reach anywhere near the bottom.

He could hear the draug tearing its way through the bush. It was moving fast and would reach him any second. There was no time to waste. It was do or die.

Having no other choice, Rowan grabbed the rope and threw his leg over the side and began climbing down as fast as he could.

As he lowered himself down, he heard the creature roar at him. Rowan looked up and saw it looking down at him. It was leaning over the edge of the cliff with part of a broken bush hanging off its head.

Rowan began climbing down the rope even faster in his desperate attempt to escape. He knew the rope wasn't long enough to reach the bottom, but he had nowhere else to go.

The creature grunted as it reached down and grabbed the rope and started hauling him up.

Rowan felt the rope being pulled up and loosened his grip to slide down it. The rope burned his hands as he desperately tried to increase the distance between him and the creature.

As the end of the rope was nearing, Rowan quickly ran out of options. He noticed a ledge on the side of the cliff and winced in pain as he tightened his grip on the rope to stop his decent. He began trying to swing himself towards the side of the cliff and was almost able to grab on to a tree root that was sticking out of the side of the ledge.

He'd be able to make it on the next swing.

The creature kept tugging on the rope, pulling him up. He had to do something now or it would have him.

Rowan let go of the rope in mid-swing and made a desperate lunge for the root that was sticking out of the side of that cliff.

Despite his best effort, he fell short of grabbing the tree root and crashed hard into the face of the cliff wall.

Rowan dropped several feet while bouncing off the protruding rocks that were sticking out of the

side of the cliff wall.  He landed hard on a small
ledge below and smacked his head on the side of a
rock.

The world went black.

# Chapter 3

Rowan woke to rain drops hitting him in the face. He slowly opened his eyes and tried to look around, but was too groggy and stiff. He saw the ledge that he had fallen on and quickly remembered where he was and what had happened.

He slowly lifted his head and felt his body aching in nearly every place.

He noticed that he was laying on the edge of the cliff's small ledge, so he carefully shifted himself away from the ledge and sat up. He felt weak and had difficulty pulling himself up.

The side of his head was painfully throbbing, along with several other parts of his body. He felt the side of his head and found dried blood. He also noticed that his hands were burnt.

He looked around hardly able to believe that he was still alive.

It looked like it was early morning. He must have been knocked unconscious for hours into the next day.  Maybe it was evening.

Fat droplets of rain were falling, but it wasn't raining hard. He wasn't soaking wet, so it must have just started sprinkling.

Alarmed, Rowan quickly looked up the cliff for any sign of the beast. It appeared to be gone and so was the rope he used to get down there in the first place.

He wasn't sure how he was going to get down. He survived the attack, but now can he survive the escape? Rowan looked down over the side of the small cliff and tried to figure out how exactly he was going to get down.

He noticed on the left side of the cliff that it sloped at such an angle that he might be able to climb down.

The rocks on the slope looked very loose. He'd have to be careful climbing down and keep his body close to the slope because of the steepness. It only went down like that for a short way until it became too steep to climb down. He would have to scoot across to the end where he could to climb down the rest of the way.

Rowan scooted to the edge and carefully slid his

body down the slope, hugging the side of the cliff wall with his body as he did so.  His bruised muscles screamed in protest.

Already some of the small rocks were starting to roll down from under him. It made him slide down with them when some of the loose dirt on the cliff wall broke free.

He tried to dig his fingers deep into the slope to prevent from sliding down any further as he continued to gingerly scoot across the cliff wall to where he could climb down.

Although he slid occasionally, everything was going as planned as he continued to make his way across. Just as he was nearing the ledge where he had planned to climb down, a rock came loose under him and caused him to slide down.

He tried to stop himself from sliding anymore by digging his fingers into the dirt and pressing his spread out body against the hillside. His efforts were in vain as he became the center of a mini rock slide that dragged him down with it.

Rowan slide down cliff and went over the side, tumbling in the air towards the ground beneath him.

He hit the top of a pine tree, which almost broke his fall, but it broke as well and he tumbled into the next branch which also broke.  Rowan bounced to the next branch below it and then to the next one below that.  He tumbled his way towards the ground through the tree, limb by limb.  Each limb either broke from him falling on it or bent and rolled him to the side to drop down to the next one below it.

He fell through the tree crashing limb to limb until landed hard on the ground with a dull thud.

Rowan hurt from just about every place on his body as he feebly laid on the ground gasping for air. The wind had been knocked out of him so times on the way down that he almost wasn't sure how to breathe again.

The tree had beaten him to a pulp, but it had also broken his fall and saved his life. He was alive and that surprised even him.

Rowan rested on the ground for a few minutes, reflecting on his luck of escaping the draug and then surviving the fall.

Twice.

His body was too sore to move yet and he was still trying to catch his breath, but he definitely felt lucky to have survived. But for how long.

After a few minutes Rowan was able to finally catch his breath and rolled to his side to look around. He was in a ravine on the mountain side. He sat up and tried to figure out which way to go.

He prided himself on having a pretty good sense of direction and he did know 'about' which way he needed to go to get back to the blacksmith's longhouse. But he'd never seen this place before and wasn't quite sure.

Below he could see where the ravine led down. It was very rocky, but not very steep.  He'd have to be careful.

It was different down here than it had been up where the draug's mound was. There was a sense of peacefulness. He could hear the birds chirping and it didn't seem as 'dead' and strange.  Plus the intense smell of rot that was near the mound wasn't present.

Rowan stood up and steadied himself. He was bruised and hurt everywhere, but he was still able to move on his own.

Surprisingly, nothing was broken.

He began making his way down the ravine, being mindful of the loose rocks as to not stumble and hurt himself any more than he already was. He knew he needed to head West, but the ravine was taking him in a more northerly direction. He figured that once he got lower and more off the mountainside, he'd be able to better recognize where he was and navigate his way back a bit better.

After walking a bit, Rowan rested a moment
when he came near the end of the ravine where it
started to level out with the rest of the hillside. He
looked back and could see where the cliff was where
he tumbled from to the ledge before falling through
the trees.

He was lucky.

Rowan got up and began to veer his path more
west in hopes of finding his way back.

He tried to stay in the clearing as much as he
could in hopes of recognizing something that would
lead him the right way.  So far nothing stood out as
familiar to him.

He tried to prevent entering the forest as much as
possible as he walked. He had foolishly lost his ax
when he threw it at the creature and was now
unarmed. He didn't want to become dinner to
wolves or anything else that lived in the forest. He'd
also heard the stories of hidden things that lived in
the forest, but never believed them before. He always
thought they were tales meant to keep children from
straying into the woods.

He was a believer in those stories now.

Rowan had been walking for most of the day and
knew he'd gone too far north.  When they had
initially gone up the mountain through the woods

following the trail left by the sheep, it had only taken them less than half a day to reach the location where the beast had been.

Rowan could tell that there was only another hour or two before the sun would set. This was not good. He had no food, water, or weapons and he was at edge of the forest. He'd have to make a decision as to what to do for the night.

Continue on or seek shelter for the night.

He didn't feel very safe going through the forest in the dark. It wasn't just because of the wolves that he was sure would be coming out for their nightly hunt;  he couldn't shake the feeling that he was being watched. He felt it all day.

As he ventured further along the way, he spotted a hollow in the ground under an old tree. It would serve as a good place to hide during the night and even offered some protection. At least he believed it would. He figured that he could crawl in and close it off with some branches to conceal the opening.

Rowan set to work immediately while he still had light to work in. He first had to check the hallow to make sure nothing else was in there. There was always the chance that it was the home of some kind of wildlife and the last thing he wanted to do was crawl in there and have a pack of angry animals attacking him.

He picked up a rock and threw it into the hole and carefully listened.

Nothing, except a crow or raven somewhere behind him that cawed loudly when it flew off which startled him.

It was too dark in the hole for him to see inside, so he picked up another rock and threw it inside. He held his breath as he listened hard for the trace of any sound or movement in the hole.

Nothing.

He was fairly confident that the hole was probably unoccupied. Rowan picked up a dead branch and put one end inside of it and shook it around in hopes of disturbing and running out anything inside. He wanted to make certain it was empty before he actually crawled in it himself.

Still nothing.

Satisfied that the hole was empty, he crawled inside.

At first he slowly lowered in his legs down inside, hoping nothing would bite them. Then he slowly lowered the rest of his body down and went inside the hallow. He felt around in the hole with his hands for anything.

It was empty and he felt confident of that now. There was always a chance something could have been in there, but didn't make a sound when he threw the rocks in.

This will serve as his hide-away for the night.

Rowan back climbed out of the hole and gathered some brush to conceal the hollow's opening while he occupied it for the night.  Once satisfied the opening was well concealed, he climbed back inside. He also found a sturdy dead limb which would serve as a club. Just in case he had to defend himself inside the hole.

It was better than having nothing at all.

Before settling, he made sure the brush in front the hole was securely in place and nested himself inside the hollow. He managed to secure his hide-away just in time before he ran out of sunlight.

Rowan laid in the hole facing the opening and stared out as he clinched the dead limb he had as a weapon. It wasn't long before his bruised and battered body was overcome by exhaustion and he drifted off to sleep.

# Chapter 4

Rowan woke to the sound of rustling leaves. The sound was coming from somewhere outside of the hole. He opened his eyes and looked out into the darkness trying to see what was out there. He wasn't able to see anything, but heard the distinctive sound of leaves crunching from a foot step.

Somebody or something was definitely out there.

He heard more leaves rustling and heavy foot steps outside in the darkness. His heart began to pound at the thought that it might be the draug creature looking for him.  He had no where to go. His hide-away for the night had now become his trap.

He sniffed the air and was reassured when he didn't smell the nauseating dead rotting flesh smell that gagged him when the creature was near.

There was a smell though, but this smell was

different.  The scent was of rancid dried sweat and dirt. It was more of a 'nasty-dirty' smell than a 'rancid-rotten' smell.  It most likely wasn't the draug, but what was it?

Rowan was still clinching tightly onto his stick awhile he peered into the darkness outside of his hole. He could hear it and smell it, but he couldn't see what it was. He started scooting forward in order to get a better look outside and see what was out there.

As he crept forward, he heard it snort as it continued taking heavily steps outside.

It was definitely something big. He could also feel the ground slightly shake with each step it took. Rowan's curiosity was now outweighing his cautiousness and he had to see what was out there.

Just as he was about the scoot forward to peer outside of the hole, he heard something softly whisper behind him.

"Don't," he heard it whisper.

Rowan froze for a second, not moving a muscle. Although startled, he wasn't quite sure that he'd actually heard anything or if it was just his imagination.

He started to move forward again.

"Don't move," he heard it whisper again in the darkness behind him. "Don't make a sound or it will find you and kill you."

Chills crawled through Rowan when he realized he wasn't just imagining it and that the whispering was coming from inside the hole behind him.

Whoever or whatever was whispering to him was in the hole with him.

Just before he was about to turn to look and try to see what was behind him talking, he sees the thing outside walk past the opening of the hollow.

Whatever it was, it was huge.

Rowan was only able to see the lower parts of its legs from just above the knees. It had to be at least three or four times taller than a tall man, maybe more. He could see that it had huge hairy feet and hairy legs.

*"It must be a giant or something," thought Rowan.*

He'd never seen a man that big in his life. He heard the stories of giants and of the gods that did battle with them. It was believed that the gods had killed them all. Occasionally there was a rumor of someone seeing one. But those reports were usually made by someone after they've had several horns of mead and were never taken seriously.

The ground slightly shook as it walked past Rowan's hidden hollow. He could only sit there in the darkness of his hole fearfully hoping that it didn't find him.

But there was also something in the hole with him.

Whatever was in the hole with him didn't seem like it was an immediate threat, however, the large man-like beast outside of the hole was another story. It seemed to be a greater of the dangers to him right now.  Rowan didn't know what to do, but he figured his chances were best if he just stayed in the hole and remain quiet.

He sat quietly hidden in the hollow listening to the large thing outside slowly walk away into the darkness.

"I think it's gone now," said whoever was hidden in the dark hollow with him.

Rowan was scared. He knew that no other human being would have possibly been able to fit in the hole with him. At least not without laying on him or being real close next to him. Either way, he felt nobody next to him. Whatever it was, it was very small.  Or something else.

"Who are you," Rowan asked.

"My name is Tom," he heard it say in the darkness, "Tom Taye."

"Who?"

"Listen very carefully," Tom said. "Stay here through the rest of the night and try not to make a sound. Only come out when you can see that the Sun has risen. When you exit this hollow, you will see some white flowers growing on a large rock. Head in that direction and stay on that course. You will have to pass through the forest, but you'll be safe in the daylight. Follow the Sun's path though the forest and you come out too far from your village."

"Wait," said Rowan, "how do you know who I am and where my village is. Who are you and what was that thing out there?"

"I told you. My name is Tom Taye. We will meet again and that thing out there was a troll. And a rather hunger one at that," he said.

"A troll," said Rowan, "I thought those things weren't real."

"I am surprised you question it after what you saw come out of that mound. Dead things aren't suppose to come back, but it chased you over a cliff didn't it? There are many unseen things out there, both good and bad. Sadly, most are bad. Well, at least for humans such as yourself," Tom said.

"You saw all of that? Who or what are you?"

"We will meet again. Follow my instructions and you will be fine."

"But how do you know all of this?"

"I must go."

Before Rowan could say anything else, the small thing that called itself Tom Taye ran out of the hole. It went so fast that Rowan only got a tiny glimpse of it in the darkness.

It looked like a tiny nude human that was probably no taller than a house cat. Unfortunately it was too dark for Rowan to get a really good look at him as he ran across the grass field giggling.

Tom Taye was extremely light footed and fast.

# Chapter 5

Rowan did what Tom had advised and stayed in the hollow for the rest of the night without making a sound. After learning that trolls were real and having one nearly discover him. Sleep was definitely out of the question, so he kept a vigilance inside the hole for the rest of the night until he saw the sun rise and announce that morning had come.

Emerging his hollow refuge, Rowan followed Tom's instructions and entered the forest.  He immediately noticed a large rock covered with white moss heather flowers ahead of him.

*"This must be the way," he thought.*

Putting the morning Sun to his back, Rowan made his way through the forest. He still had the stick that he'd armed himself with during the night and was using it as a walking stick. His body was wary and beaten.  He hadn't really rested in a few days nor eaten.

He felt weak from injury, fatigue, and hunger.

Remembering the honey biscuit that he had wrapped and tucked inside his shirt, he stopped walking and dropped his walking stick on the ground.  Quickly he reached inside his shirt and felt around for the biscuit.

It wasn't there!

He pulled his shirt out and shook it, hoping the wrapped honey biscuit would drop to the ground.

It was gone!  He must have lost it when he fell off the cliff.

Rowan was openly disappointed. He fixed his shirt and stared blankly ahead.  Looking around the area, he could see what looked like golden flowers. It was the tell tale signs of what was probably chanterelle. He picked up his stick and began walking towards them.

He could already smell their fruity aroma as he got closer tot hem. They were definitely the edible yellow mushrooms that he was hoping they'd be.

Rowan rejoiced. He wasn't finished just yet.

His stomach gurgled as he picked them. He had no means to make a fire and cook them so he ate them raw as he picked them.

To his surprise, they tasted very peppery. They

weren't sweet tasting like they smelled and also were very chewy.  He had them before but he wasn't really sure if they were safe to eat raw,. His hunger overrode his wisdom and he gobbled a few of them down.

He only ate enough of them until his hunger subsided, but already his stomach was starting to feel ill and now he wondered if he should have even eaten any of them.

*"So this is how it ends."*

He knew some mushrooms were poisonous and hoped he hadn't been foolish and allowed his hunger to seal his doom. His stomach was upset, but he wasn't really very ill from it. Although not feeling at his best, he felt confident that he'd be okay and proceeded with his trek through the forest.

As he walked through the forest, he made sure he kept his direction true by checking the Sun now and again.  For some odd reason, he felt the little man's direction would be true.

Because of the mushrooms, he did have to stop every so often to let his stomach settle. He wasn't really ill and he didn't feel nauseated, but he sure felt uneasy.

It was when he had stopped to lean against his walking stick and let his stomach settle that he heard something rustling in the trees behind him.

His heart beat began to quicken when he thought of the troll.  He tried to remember the tales he'd heard about trolls. Did they never came out in the daylight? Daylight was bad for them, wasn't it?  He couldn't remember why, but he remembered that trolls absolutely could not come out in the daylight. The Sun did something very bad to them, he was sure he remembered that part right.

Because the Sun was out, it most likely wasn't a troll. But something was there. He heard it.

Cautiously, he slowly turned and looked around at the trees behind him.

Nothing was nothing there.

At least he didn't see anything. That didn't mean nothing was there. Maybe it was that wee Tom Taye character that had helped him avoid the troll last night and told him the way to get back.

He decided to call out.

"Tom? Is that you? Tom Taye!?"

Rowan listened for any kind of response, but got none. He listened for a moment but only heard the occasional bird or breeze blowing through the trees above.

Maybe it was just his imagination.

Rowan continued walking through the forest. It wasn't but moments later when he heard it again. But it wasn't just the rustling of leaves that he heard this, but what also sounded like footsteps.

They didn't sound like footsteps made by a human walking. They were too soft and sounded different. They sounded more like a deer's steps.

Rowan stopped again and turned towards the sounds to look and listen, but again he saw and heard nothing.

Something was in the forest following him, he was certain that. He looked around the trees from where he thought the sound had came, but found nothing. He searched for any sign of something hiding in the foliage.

As he looked around, he couldn't help reflecting on the fact that there certainly seemed to be many things in the forest that were out to get him. He couldn't believe it. All the stories that he heard about the various creatures living in the woods. Stories that he thought were just meant to keep children from wandering off in the forest and getting lost. The stories were about things that actually existed after all.

He stood and listened intently for a moment and still heard nothing but the wind and the birds.

He decided to proceed on his way, but this time with a quicker pace. Apparently whatever it was that seemed to be following him wasn't going to show itself.  It was best just to get through the forest as quickly as possible.

The Sun had passed over him as he continued making its way west. According to Tom's directions, it shouldn't be that much further.

Quite frankly, he couldn't wait to get out of the forest. The drab life of a blacksmith's thrall wasn't nearly so bad after all, considering everything that's happened in the past few days.  At least as a thrall he rarely had to venture out into the wilderness where things were set on killing him.

He remembered the blacksmith and his son.

They were dead.

Life wouldn't return to how it was before this had all happened. What was to become of him? Who in their right mind would believe him when he told them what had happened. He knew that he wouldn't believe such a story.  Especially such a tail when it was told by a thrall. They would probably suspect that he'd murdered his master in an attempt to escape his servitude.

Surely he would be put to death for murder.

Rowan's wandering mind was quickly silenced when he heard the footsteps again. It was like a trot and it was now off to his left.

He didn't stop to listen this time and picked up his pace until he was at a half run himself. His heart also picked up the pace and was beating in rhythm to his steps.

He continued his quick pace and pretended not to notice the trotting off to the left of him. He tried not look in its direction, for fear that it would try to hide out of sight from him again.

He had to get a look and see what it was.

Rowan did his best to look in the corner of his eye and see what it was without turning his head..

In the back of his mind he was hoping it would just be a deer. But obviously that would be asking too much for it to be something normal and ordinary.

Besides, there was nothing ordinary about a deer trotting beside a human anyways.

Rowan finally did catch a glimpse of in the corner of his eye and caught a sight of what appeared to be a woman with long flowing hair.

He also thought she was nude, but couldn't be sure.

He stopped abruptly in his tracks to get a good look at her, but she had already disappeared in the trees. She was once again was out of sight.  Rowan looked in the direction that he thought she'd gone. He could still hear her moving through the trees and it sounded like she was trotting instead of running.

*"My imagination is definitely playing games with me,"* he thought, *"probably because of those stupid mushrooms."*

He was also fairly sleep deprived.  But this wasn't his imagination.

The sound faded off and Rowan took a quick look around him to make sure nothing else was there.

Feeling satisfied that he was once again alone, and perhaps the trotting was nothing but a deer with his mind playing tricks on him, rowan set off again. It may have been something else, but it didn't matter. He had to get out of the forest.

His stomach had finally settled down and his shaken nerves had given him a sense of renewed energy.  Getting out of the forest was his main priority and he kept his pace quickened.

He was determined to let nothing stop him from getting out of the forest.

Rowan had kept the pace up for quite a bit until he began feeling tired from it.  He could see a clearing ahead, which meant that he was finally about to come out of the forest.

He was relieved and a little bit excited.

Even though he was exhausted, he decided not to rest and continued walking.  There was no sense in resting now.  He was determined to get to the clearing and out of the forest.

Rowan heard someone giggling behind him.

He abruptly stopped walking and just stood there frozen in his tracks. He remained motionless and listened.

He heard it again. It was a female's giggle.

Reluctantly Rowan turned around to look in the direction he heard the giggling and was surprised to see a woman's face peering at him from behind a tree.

It was the same woman that he thought he'd seen earlier in the woods, but thought his mind was playing tricks on him.  Perhaps it was playing tricks on him now.

Even though he wasn't sure if what he'd seen earlier was real or not, he was sure that what he seeing now was.

He looked at lady in the forest bewildered and dumbfounded. She had long curly blonde hair that fell over her shoulders. Her hair covered her shoulders and the rest of her body was hidden behind a tree.  Rowan still wasn't sure if she was nude or not, but her shoulders and arms were bare.

*"What's a woman doing out here in the forest?"*

She just looked at him and smiled as she giggled again.

She was beautiful, perhaps the most beautiful woman that he'd ever seen. That is, of what he could see of her.

Realizing that he must be near the village and that this was probably just someone who he'd never seen before, Rowan relaxed his guard a bit. Maybe she's a visitor from another village and has lost her way.

He was just about to ask her who she was and if he was near the village when he spotted something most peculiar about her.

*"Was that a tail?"*

He saw what looked like a cow's tail swish behind her.  As quickly as he saw it swish in the air, it was hidden again from sight behind the tree.

She giggled and reached her arm out to him,

beckoning him to come nearer to her.

Temptation was overwhelming, he couldn't help feeling extremely attracted to her and he didn't know why.

But he hadn't forgotten about everything else that had happened so far and thought better of it. She seemed friendly, but that didn't mean anything out here in the forest. Besides, why was she hiding behind the tree? It could be a trap.  Rowan decided to play it cool and be as polite as he could.

"I apologize, but I am in a hurry," he said, "I bid you a good day."

He didn't feel right about the whole thing, so he quickly turned and walked away.

Rowan kept his quickened pace the rest of the way out of the forest. He did, however, carefully listen as he walked to make sure she wasn't following him.

He wasn't quite sure if she was following or not, but he was too afraid to physically look back. His instincts told him not to look back and to just keep going without stopping.

His mind raced and he tried not to panic as he kept his brisk pace to get out of the forest as quickly as possible.

*"She was beautiful and probably naked," he thought, "but why would she be naked and why was she hiding herself behind the tree? And was that a tail he saw swishing behind her?"*

She didn't seem to be following him, but he didn't hear her run off either.

To his joy he finally came out of the forest and reached the clearing. He could see the fjord below and recognized the hillsides in the distance.

He knew where he was now and he wasn't too far away.

Without taking the chance of looking back in the direction of where the lady in the forest was, Rowan began walking down the green rocky hillside towards the narrow fjord. He knew the fjord would lead him directly to the Blacksmith's tall thatched mossy roofed longhouse.

# Chapter 6

Rowan trekked down the hillside and passed through a few patches of woods as he made his way towards the fjord. By time the sun was beginning to set, he'd finally made it to the outskirts of the village.

The blacksmith's longhouse was just on the other side.

He rested on a log at the edge of a wood line overlooking the village and pondered how best to proceed on. He needed to inform the Blacksmith's family as to what had happened to the Bjord and Sven.

The Jarl would also have to be informed.

But he didn't know exactly how to handle any of that. Of course he knew they wouldn't take it very well. But also, would they even believe him?

Rowan figured it would also be best to go around the village settlement and make his way to the blacksmith's longhouse. This way he could avoid everyone else and not have to explain himself or have to answer where his master Bjord was to anyone except Gwenda.

He felt because of what happened the other night with the cat and sheep, she'd probably be the only one who'd believe him.

Feeling rest enough, Rowan began making his way around the village towards the longhouse. He tried to keep out of sight by staying inside the edge of the woods.

"Thrall! Where's your master the Blacksmith?"

Someone had called out to him. Already, his plans have been foiled.

Rowan stopped dead in his tracks, turned and looked in the direction of the voice.

He recognized the man.

It was Oleg, one of the karls from the village. Rowan didn't notice him when he was walking through. Oleg had been quietly sitting on a tree he'd just felled, taking a rest.

"I asked you a question thrall," Oleg said, "where's your master?"

Rowan's heart began to race. He didn't know what to do or how to answer. It was the very question he was intentionally trying to avoid until he'd at least spoken to Gwenda first.

Oleg stood up holding his chopping ax and angrily asked again.

"Answer me thrall!"

Rowan looked down at the ground and quietly said, "he was killed on the mountain by a beast."

Raising an eyebrow in disbelief, Oleg stood there for a moment and looked at Rowan.

"Come with me."

He pointed his ax at Rowan and then towards the village.

"Walk," he said, "go thrall."

Rowan obediently turned and began walking towards the village. He had no choice really. If he refused the demand of a karl, one of the village's freemen, he'd be cut down by the man's ax.

There was a difference between a thrall, who was property, and that of a freeman. It is not considered murder to kill a thrall. There's only the obligation to reimburse the thrall's owner the weregeld for damaging their property.  It was no different than killing a cow or breaking a tool and reimbursing the owner amount of the property's value.

They walked the whole way without saying a word.

Oleg rested his ax on his shoulder as he walked behind Rowan. They walked this way until they reached the village and continued towards the Jarl's Hall.

They gathered an occasional curious look from some of the villagers who took noticed them of them passing.

They stopped when they reached the village center where the Jarl's Hall was located. The great hall were Jarl Erling resided. Rowan had never been inside. He'd been to the village center many times and even to the Jarl's Hall, but was always told to wait outside. The Hall was a place for karls. The only thralls allowed in without their masters were the Jarl's own thralls.

This time Rowan got to go in and see what it looked like inside for the first time. Oleg pushed him inside.

"Go in," he said, "go inside.

Rowan stumbled in the doorway and nearly tripped. He paused momentarily as his eyes adjusted to the lighting inside.

He was surprised by the Hall's size. It looked

even bigger from the inside than it did from the outside. The design was very different than the typical longhouse. It was much larger and more open to accommodate a larger group of people.

There were three great fire pits in the center of the Jarl's Hall. Each fire pit had heavy wooden tables and benches lined on each side of them. Along the walls were additional rows of heavy tables which also had benches on each side.

On the opposite end of the Hall in the center was an elaborately carved wooden chair raised up above the others which sat Jarl Erling seated with housekarls armed with spears at guard on either side of him.

Rowan knew what the Jarl looked like, he'd seen him before.  The Jarl had requested items to be made by the blacksmith on numerous occasions. Bjord crafted many of the weapons that were carried by the Jarl's Housekarl Guard.

Oleg grabbed Rowan by the iron collar he wore around his neck and used it to lead him through the Hall to where the Jarl was seated.

When they reached the Jarl and stood before him, Oleg pulled Rowan down by the iron collar.

"On your knees thrall!"

Rowan kept his eyes lowered and knelt down before the Jarl, who was looking on with great curiosity.

"My lord," said Oleg, "I found this thrall outside the village. I asked him where his master was and he claims that he's been killed by a wild beast."

Jarl Erling nodded without saying a word and looked at Rowan.

"My lord,' said Oleg, "we haven't seen the blacksmith in a couple days and I suspect this thrall has killed his master and his son."

The Jarl continued to quietly look at Rowan for a few more moments before he finally turned towards one of the guards standing next to him.

"Bind him."

The housekarl stepped forward, handed his spear to the other guard, and pulled out some leather lashings from his belt. Oleg kicked Rowan forward onto his face while the guard bound his hands behind him.

After he secured the binding, the guard pulled Rowan up by his arm and lifted him up to his feet.

"Secure him for now," said the jarl.

The guard guided Rowan to a support beam near one of the large fire pits and pulled him down to his knees while he fastened Rowan's neck collar to a chain connected to the wood beam.

"Fetch the blacksmith's wife," said the jarl to the housekarl standing next to him.

The guard handed the other guard his spear back and left the hall.

Rowan remained there on his knees chained to the beam with his hands bound behind him. He was not sure of what was going to happen to him. But he was definitely not a very good predicament.

He questioned his decision to return.

The Jarl's hall gradually began filling up with some of the karls from the village. They were curious about the thrall and what was going on.

Rowan could hear them murmuring different theories amongst themselves. It wasn't looking good for him. He heard several of them suggesting that he be put to death.

A man called Thorn stood up on his bench and addressed the entire hall.

"I demand justice for my brother Bjord and my nephew Sven," he said, "justice that this thrall be put to death for his crimes of murder."

Rowan was horrified when heard him say this. It was exactly what he feared might happen. He did not do anything wrong, but how in the world would he prove it.

Oleg quickly stood up on the bench he was seated on.

"I take claim to this thrall," he said.

"How do you have the right to take claim of my brother's property?"

"I take claim by law for finding the master-less thrall after he slayed his master," Oleg said. "He no longer has a master and belongs to the first one to take claim of him."

"That is nonsense," said Thorn. "The thrall, and any other property that belonged to Bjord, would be passed to Bjord's heirs."

"There aren't any legal heirs," said Oleg.

"There are so," said Thorn.

"The blacksmith's only heir was Sven and he is dead," said Oleg.

"Sven was not his son and he was not the only heir," said Thorn, "I am his brother and I have claim."

"That does not make you an heir and without any heirs his property is up for grabs."

"Nothing is up for grabs," said Thorn, "the

murderer will be put to death for his crimes and will be claimed by no one!"

"Calm down," said the jarl, "calm down!"

Jarl Erling stood up and calmly quietened the men in the hall.

"We're not even sure yet if Bjord and his son are even dead or not. Let us hear from his household first to verify."

The bickering between the men halted for the moment. The jarl turned and whispered something in the ear of one of guards and then sat back down as the man quickly headed out the door.

The chatter in the hall gradually became louder and louder as more men continued coming in to find out what was going on.

The men in the hall fell silent when the blacksmith's wife showed up along with her mother at the door. Gwenda and Helga made their way past the gawking eyes of the men inside to where the jarl sat waiting for them.

Helga gave Rowan a puzzled look before looking at Gwenda then up at Jarl Erling.

"My lord," said Gwenda, "why have you summoned us to your hall?"

"Woman," said the jarl, "where is your husband

and son."

"My lord," she said. "they went into the forest up the mountainside a couple days ago.  They left with our thrall, the three of them."

"A couple days ago with your thrall? Why did they go into the forest?"

"My lord, we had been awakened in the middle of the night by a screeching cat and the sound of our livestock panicking."

"You woke to the sound of panicking livestock?"

"Yes my lord, our sheep were panic stricken and had gotten out of their pens. They ran out through the door and escaped outside."

"What frightened them?"

"We never saw what caused them to become so afraid," she said, "but our thrall said that a strange cat had chased them."

"A strange cat?"

"Yes, my lord. Our thrall said there was a cat that woke him by sitting on his chest and that it was trying to crush him. He said when he got the cat off of him that it went howling after our livestock."

She looked around at the faces of the men in the hall. Many of them had puzzled looks on their faces and were shaking their heads in disbelief.

"It went howling after your livestock," said Jarl Erling. "Ignore them and please continue."

"Yes my lord," she said. "We ran outside to fetch the frightened sheep in the darkness, but they had already ran into the forest."

"In the darkness?  How did you know they ran into the forest?"

"We could hear them screaming as they ran. It was too dark to see them, but we could hear them."

"Did you go into the forest to gather them?"

"No my lord, it was too dark, so my husband decided to track them first thing in the morning."

"And did he?"

"When morning came, my husband, my son, and our thrall set out into the forest to find the sheep and bring them back."

"And that was the last time you'd heard from any of them?"

"Yes, my lord," she said, "that was the last time we had heard from any of them. Until now."

"Until now?"

"Yes, my lord, until now."

She turned and pointed at Rowan.

"This is the first time we have seen our thrall since then," she said, "but what of my son and my husband? It has been three days since we've seen or heard from them."

Helga stood next to her and sadly nodded.

"The thrall must be put to death for murder," said Oleg. "The blacksmith's household deserves justice!"

Several of the men in the hall shouted in agreement. Rowan could feel a lump forming in his throat as he became more and more concerned for his health.

Things began getting louder in hall as accusations flew until the Jarl had to finally stand up and quieten them down.

Once the hall became quiet again he looked down at Rowan who was kneeling on the ground still chained to the beam with a worried look on his face.

"Tell us thrall," he said, "what happened to your master?"

"Who cares what the thrall has to say," said Oleg, "he..."

"Silence!" said Jarl Erling. "We don't even know what happened. There is only speculation at this point. We will give him a chance to tell us what

94

happened and then we will check his story."

Jarl Erling looked back at Rowan and approached him, touching him on the shoulder.

"Tell us what happened when you went looking for the sheep," he said. "Tell us everything that happened."

"Yes my lord," Rowan said. "Like my mistress Gwenda said, I woke up in the middle of the night because there was a cat sitting in my chest making it hard for me to breath. It wasn't a normal cat, because it quickly became as heavy as a full grown man. Its weight was crushing my chest and I couldn't breathe. It kept getting heavier and heavy and seemed to also get bigger and bigger."

"This is utter nonsense," someone shouted.

He was quickly hushed by other men in the hall before the jarl needed to bother intervening.

"Continue thrall," said Jarl Erling.

"The cat had me trapped under its weight and I could no longer breathe. When I tried to get it off, it howled and jumped off of me."

"It released you?"

"Yes, my lord," said Rowan. "That's when it chased after the sheep."

"What did it do to the sheep?"

"It screeched and frightened them until they ran out of the longhouse and into the forest."

"You saw them run into the forest?"

"No my lord. I saw the cat chase them out the door. It was my master Bjord that saw them run into the forest."

"Where was he to have seen this?"

"He grabbed a torch and ran outside after them," Rowan said.

Jarl Erling turned and looked at Gwenda and Helga, who were nodding their heads in agreement.

"What happened after that," asked Jarl Erling, "was he able to gather any of them back?"

"We left first thing the very next morning to track the sheep in the forest. We tracked them up the mountain to a hidden burial mound that we discovered."

"A hidden burial mound," said the jarl. "What?"

The hall grew louder as men began talking between themselves, some arguing.

"Silence," said the jarl. "Be quiet so we can hear this! Thrall, what burial mound?"

"My lord," said Rowan, "The burial mound we found following the trail left behind by the sheep."

"I know of no burial mound in the forest near here," the jarl said.

"He's making up a story to cover his crimes," Oleg said.

"We were attacked by a large creature there," said Rowan.

"A bear?" asked the jarl.

"No, my lord. Much worse. It was some kind of dead creature. It was bigger than a man and stronger than a bear. It killed Bjord and then it killed Sven."

"Nonsense!"

Jarl Erling turned and gave Oleg a stern look.

"I'll have no more of those outbursts from you," he said. "Thrall, continue. If it killed your master and his son, then how did you manage to escape in one piece?"

"I escaped by running and climbing down a cliff. I got down to the other side side and hid in the forest."

Oleg lifted his arms up in the air and said nothing.

"So you ran like a coward and left them to die,"

the jarl said.

"No my lord," Rowan said, "they were already dead.  We battled the creature, but we were not able to inflict any kind of damage to it. Except..."

"Except what?"

"Except when I was able to put Bjord's ax into its back. It appeared to be burned by it."

"Appeared to be burned by it," said the jarl. "What do you mean?"

"My lord, when the ax was embedded in its back, I could see smoke coming from the wound. It looked like the ax was really hurting it and it struggled to remove it."

"It you were hurting it," said the jarl, "then how come you didn't slay it?"

"I didn't have a weapon and I did not think I would be able to kill it, my lord. I did the only thing I could think to do."

"You ran?"

Many of the men in the hall began laughing.

"Of course he ran, he's just a thrall," said someone in the hall.

"I ran," said Rowan, "but the beast gave chase. The beast was fast and I knew I wouldn't be able to outrun it, so I climbed down the side of the cliff. That was how I escaped it."

"And now you are here," said the jarl, "with this story."

"I spent the next day finding my way back. That was when Oleg found me, when I was on my way to the blacksmith's house to tell them what had happened."

The men in the Jarl's Hall grew loud again arguing their opinions about what happened.

Oleg stepped forward.

"My lord," he said, "you don't believe this thrall's story do you? It is obvious that he has made up a tale to cover up his crime."

"There may be truth to the thrall Rowan's tale," said raspy loud voice near door.

It was the village's lawspeaker, Alvis the wise. The old man had quietly come in and been listening to the whole story.

He made his way through the other men to the other side of the hall with the assistance of his staff aiding him as he walked.

"What say you lawspeaker?" asked Jarl Erling.

When the old man had his way to him, he

motioned one of the guards to fetch a chair for the old man to seat himself.

After being brought a chair, the lawspeaker sat down.

"There has been talk of something dreadful lurking in the mountain side for a few years. Stories that men have told when they ventured too deep in the forest when hunting."

"Those are just tales!" someone said.

The lawspeaker nodded and said, "yes, tales they are, but none the less they all seem to say the same thing."

"And what is that?"

"There is a draug in the mountain forest."

"A draug?" said the jarl.

"Draugs are just stories told to scare children," one man said.

"What is a draug, wise lawspeaker," asked the jarl.

"What is said of draugs is that they the dead who have come back to walk again. It is said that they have the power to shape shift into other creatures and it has also been said that they will try to crush someone in their sleep by growing."

100

"Sorcery!" yelled someone from the hall.

"Perhaps," said the law-speaker, "but we don't really know what they are. I haven't heard of a draug since I was a young boy."

"That was in an age before time itself!" said someone.

Laughter erupted in the hall.

The law-speaker when silent, he didn't find the joke funny at all.

After much of the laughter died down, Jarl Erling walked back and stepped up to his chair.

"We will send a group of men to investigate this burial mound and see if what the thrall claims is true."

"We know it's not true," said Oleg, "this is nonsense. There are no monsters in the forest. This thrall killed his master and his master's son and needs to be put to death for it."

There was a load roar of agreement from many of the other men in the hall.

"We will investigate this matter by sending a group of men to see for ourselves," the jarl said. "The thrall will lead them to the mound."

The hall grew loud again as some of the men

protested.

"Silence!" said Jarl Erling. "If there is any proof of wrongdoing by this thrall, then he will be brought back to this hall and be put to death in accordance to our laws."

A few men shook their heads in disagreement, but it was the jarl's decision and that was the end of it. They had no choice but to accept it.

"I will also say this," announced the jarl as he sat down, "if there is any truth to the thrall's story, then we shall have to do something about the creature."

There was a general agreement to this resolution, however many expressed their protests because they didn't believe in such a creature and that thrall was doing nothing but creating a story to save his own hide. The men argued between themselves until the hall got so loud, the Jarl had enough.

"I will need some men to go up the mountain," said the jarl. "They will be guided by the thrall first thing tomorrow morning to investigate if there is any truth to his story."

Nobody stepped forward and the hall became quiet.

"It will be your chance to see for yourselves," he pointed out. "Why aren't there any brave men to stepping forward? I thought none of you believed in such creatures.  After all, this thrall that I've heard some of you repeatedly call a coward has faced this beast and survived," Jarl Erling mocked.

"That is only because his story is not true," said Oleg.

"Then you volunteer?"

Oleg did not answer.

Several of the other men, having had their courage questioned, stepped up and proudly proclaimed that they'd go.

The Jarl took five of the karls from the village who volunteered and an additional three of his own Housekarl Guard to accompany them.

"At tomorrow's sunrise," announced the jarl, "the thrall Rowan will guide these men to the exact location in order to verify his story. Until then, this matter is close for the night."

One of the jarl's guards unfastened the chain Rowan was connected to and moved him to the corner of the hall. He was then chained to a support beam near the back corner of the hall.

One of the jarl's thralls had given Rowan a meager meal of porridge and some water. Having not eaten for a couple days, save a few raw wild mushrooms that made him feel ill, he was very appreciative.

It didn't take long until exhaustion took over and Rowan fell asleep.

# Chapter 7

The morning came fast and Rowan woke to someone kicking his foot.

"Get up."

He looked up and saw Hakon standing in front of him.  Hakon was the captain of the Jarl's Housekarl Guard.

"Get up, thrall."

Rowan scrambled to get up to his feet. He immediately noticed the soreness in his body and found himself moving slower than he wanted.

The housekarl unchained him from the beam and removed the leather lashing that was used to bind his hands.

Rowan was relieved to have his hands untied. It wasn't tied very tight, but his hands still went numb. Not to mention how difficult it was sleeping, to be bound like that.

He rubbed his wrists to let the blood flow through them again.

"I am not going to bother tethering you," Hakon said. "I trust you're not going to try to run off."

He patted the hilt of his sword hanging from his belt.

Rowan got the message and nodded.

He led Rowan outside where the rest of the men had already gathered and were preparing themselves.  It wasn't long before they were ready to go.

Some of them were armed with swords and spears, while some carried battle axes. A couple of the men carried bows and quivers of arrows.

They were well armed.

Nevertheless, Rowan quietly didn't think they were prepared for what was up on that hill. He escaped last time and knew it was pure luck on his part; and this time he was unarmed.

"We need to see where the trail started and follow the same path that they did," he said. "Thrall, show us where you and your master entered the forest."

They walked to the edge of the forest next to the blacksmith's longhouse and Rowan showed them the path leading into the forest where the sheep had ran.

"This is it?"

"Yes," said Rowan, "they ran through here and up the hillside."

"Okay," said Hakon, "keep your eyes open. Thrall, lead the way."

They walked into the forest and up the hill following the path as Rowan led the way. The trail left wasn't as prominent as it was before, so Rowan had to also rely on memory and hope.

Mostly hope.

He hoped that he was taking them the right way. If he wasn't able to lead them to the mound where Bjord and Sven had been killed, then it would definitively be his death sentence.

They walked through the woods for a couple hours until they came upon the remnants of the first sheep.

This was the same one found by Bjord, but there wasn't much left of it this time. Something had discovered it and had made a feast. There was just its head, some scattered bone, and its hide left.  It was hard to tell that it was one of the sheep.

The sight of this pleased Rowan because it told him that they were going the right way. This was a small glimmer of hope that he'd be able to prove his story and spare his life.

The men only paused briefly for a swig from a skin of mead that they passed around and then Rowan continued leading them up through the woods.

Having gained confidence that he was going the right way, the led them with a quicker pace.  It wasn't long until they came to the spot where the other sheep's body laid.

Again it was obvious that wildlife had discovered the it and had eaten most of it. There was only the sheep's head and a few bones left on this one. The remains reassured Rowan that he was still leading them in the right direction. His biggest fear of this whole expedition was going the wrong way and getting them lost.

As they continued further up the hill, the smell of decay began filling the air around them.

It was the same strangely strong and extremely rancid odor that Rowan had smelled before.  One of the karls abruptly dropped his shield and spear on the ground, and then dropped to his knees and lost his last meal.

He quickly recovered and picked up his things. Nobody said a word and kept going. The smell got even stronger as they progressed further up the hill.

A couple of the other men had occasionally stopped to gag when the odor became too overpowering. There was a couple times when Rowan wasn't sure if they were getting sick because of the smell or from seeing the other man get sick. Or if it were a combination of both, because as soon as one guy lost it, another quickly followed.

The smell of decay definitely had their attention. This time Rowan wasn't as bothered by the smell as he was before. He was more bothered by knowing what the smell belonged to.

The odor meant the draug was near.

A few of the men were starting to get concerned and one of them said, "what if the thrall isn't lying? Are we prepared for what we will find up there?"

"We're prepared," said Hakon, "We will make our stand no matter what is up there."

The rest of the men nodded in agreement, not wanting to reveal their own feelings of apprehension or show any sign of weakness.

The smell grew even stronger as they made their way up the hill. A few of the men were now trying to cover their mouths in an attempt to not breath in the putrid scent and allow it to sicken them any more. It was hard for them not to feel like their stomachs weren't about to turn on them at any moment. In fact, Rowan thought the odor was a little bit stronger than it was the last time he'd been through there.

Not wanting to alarm them any more than they already were, he kept that observation to himself.

Just as the eyes of some of the men's were starting to water from the putrid smell, they reached the thicket that led to the cliff where Rowan climbed down when the creature chased him.

"This is where the sheep tracks ended." Rowan said. "We figured that the sheep probably ran themselves through this bush and ran over the cliff that's on the other side."

"That's a big hole for sheep," said on man.

"The hole through the bushes was much smaller. The creature made it bigger."

Rowan pointed to the now larger hole through the bushes.

"This is also where I escaped the creature."

The draug had smashed its way through the bushes and made a large enough hole to walk through now.

Rowan walked over to the ledge and noticed the rope he used to lower himself down was on the ground by the cliff's edge. He pointed at the rope.

"There's the rope I used," Rowan said. "It's still tied to the root of the bush I tied it to when I lowered myself down to escape the creature. It grabbed the rope and then started to pull me up. That was when I was forced to let go and fall to the edge of a small cliff below."

Rowan carefully looked over the side looking for where he landed.

One of the men picked up the rope and then looked over the side of the cliff below.

"I don't believe this," he said, "there is no way he would have survived such a fall."

"You're holding the rope," said Hakon.

"He could have just left this here to make his story look real," he said, tossing the rope on the ground.

"Where is this so-called creature," one man asked.

The thought of the creature made Rowan turn pale. He absolutely did not want to go back up there. Especially to go back up there unarmed where the beast was probably waiting for them. He could smell its putrid odor.  He knew it was somewhere close.

While the men were still examining where Rowan turned and walked back through the torn brush and pointed to the path torn through the brush that was further up the hill.

"The mound where the creature came at us is through there. It's also where Bjord and Sven's bodies should still be."

"For your sake, you better be right."

"For all our sake," said another man, "I hope he is wrong."

It was now becoming obvious to some of the men that Rowan had told them the truth in the Jarl's Hall. They could see where the bushes and tree branches had been torn away by something that was much larger than a man.

They walked up to where a path was torn through the bushes and examined it.

"A bear perhaps?"

"No," said Hakon, "that was no bear."

Rowan pointed through the passageway and said, "the mound where the beast attacked us is right through there. It is just on the other side of the path."

The men who were previously doubtful took on a new stance. They raised their shields and had their weapons at the ready for anything that would come through the torn passageway.

Rowan, being unarmed and unwilling, stood behind them.

He hoped the men would be able to successful battle the creature and kill it. But he had doubt in that. He'd seen the beast in action and knew these men were no threat to it.

The passageway, which was barely wide enough for one man to pass through when Bjord had originally hacked his way through, was now wide enough for three men to pass side by side. This was all thanks to the beast crashing its way through when it was chasing after Rowan.

The men grouped up three men wide and made a shield wall with their weapons poised as they carefully began stepping forward through the passageway.

The remaining men packed behind them with their weapons at the ready. The two men with bows each nocked an arrow and had them partially drawn back, ready to fire over the heads of the men in front of them.

Rowan tailed behind them a pace or two. He

knew what laid ahead waiting and he was glad he was in the back of everyone. He didn't want to go through, but even though nobody said anything, he knew he had to pass through with them to the other side.

The men got through without incident and took up positions in front of the mound. They were not sure what to expect, except from what Rowan told them had happened.

"There is Bjord."

The body of Bjord still laid where the beast had killed him.

Hakon walked over to investigate the body. The rest of the men continued looking around with their weapons at the ready.  They did not want to turn their backs to the mound.

They now believed Rowan's story completely and were now visibly shaken.

Hakon knelt down and looked at Bjord's body and examining it. After a few moments, he stood back up.

"This was not done by any man. You can tell his body was crushed by something very large, but not a bear."

"How do you know it was not a bear?"

"I've seen the body of someone who has lost his fight with a bear," said Hakon. "This is different."

One of the other housekarls walked over by Hakon to inspect Bjord's body himself.

"That was done by something unnatural," he said.

Hakon turned around and looked towards Rowan, who was still standing by the hole through the bushes.

"Where's the body of his son, Sven?"

"The creature threw his body over the side of the cliff," Rowan said as he pointed in the direction of the ledge.

The two men walked to the ledge Rowan had pointed to and looked over the side.  They nodded at each other before returning to where the rest of the men were near the mound.

"Do you see him," asked Hakon.

They both shook their heads.

Hakon looked at Rowan and asked, "where did the creature come out from?"

"I don't know. He was just suddenly there upon us."

Incidentally, just as he said this, a mist began coming out from around the burial mound.

"A mist just like this formed before it appeared," said Rowan as he pointed towards the mound.

He had forgotten about the mist until now.

"Shield Wall!"

The men quickly assembled next to each other tightly and formed a wall by overlapping their shields together side by side and held their weapons at the ready above their shields.

Rowan nervously stood behind them, unarmed.

The mist grew thicker around them as did the putrid smell of death and decay in the air. It was a smell nobody could ever become accustomed to.

The two men with bows drew back on their strings, ready to fire their arrows immediately at the first sign of anything.

When the mist grew too thick to see through was when they were startled by the ear piercing screech of the dead walker suddenly appeared behind them.

The men quickly turned around and tried to reform their shield wall in the opposite direction.

They were too late.

The massive angry beast charged at them while swinging its massive arms.

It knocked Rowan to the side and caused him to

tumble in the air as it charged past him towards the bowmen.

Rowan hit the ground hard and nearly rolled off the cliff's edge where Sven had met his death just days ago.

The creature knocked both bowmen backwards as it charged through them.  The blow caused them to misfire their bows and release their arrows harmlessly into the air.

With a ferocious charge, it hit the line of men and bashed three of them back several feet onto their backs while they were tried to reform their shield wall.

The creature turned towards one man and tore the spear out of his hands while pounding his fist down on his head.  The man's legs gave way from under him and he slumped the ground, dead.

The creature's strength was as unnatural as its rage.

It roared in pain when a man drove his spear into its back while another man thrust his sword into it. The monstrosity swung around and grabbed the man's arm he swung his sword for another hit.

The fiend then flung the man off to the side, causing him to tumble feebly to the side as another man swung his ax down upon the beast and sunk it in the shoulder.

The beast angrily punched through the man's shield and caused it the shatter, spraying wood splinters in the air. The beast swung with its other arm and hit him in the chest so powerfully that crushed his chest.

The ax wielder fell back a couple feet and dropped to his knees before spitting out blood as he fell to the ground.

The other men swung their weapons, but kept some distance trying not to get hit by the extremely powerful swings of its arms.

Rowan eased himself away from the ledge and got up from the ground. He took a couple steps backward looking at the cliff that he was almost swatted over and then noticed Bjord's ax..

It was laying on the ground hidden in the tall grass. The creature must have pulled it free and tossed it there.

Rowan picked it up off the ground and made his way to join the men fighting. He wasn't sure if it was really a good idea to try fight the creature or take the opportunity to run for it.

He decided to fight.

The men kept getting knocked back as the wounds they inflicted on the beast appeared to be useless.

Hakon was hit so hard that he had actually dropped his sword as he fell backward into Rowan, taking them both to the ground.  Hakon's shield already had been shattered from one of the creature's strikes and discarded just moments before.

The housekarl laid on the ground for a moment choking. His breath that had been knocked out of him by the hit.

Rowan scrambled back to his feet and picked Bjord's ax up.  He stepped around Hakon and began to approach the beast with the intent of striking it with all his might.

Hakon grabbed his leg and stopped him.

"No," he said, "it is useless. Run!"

Rowan lowered the ax and looked at him, not entirely believing what he'd just heard.

Hakon picked up his sword and rose to his feet.

"It's useless men!  Run! Run for your very lives!"

He lunged forward and grabbed one of the fighting men by the shoulder and shoved him towards the pathway.  "Run, I said!"

The remaining men stopped fighting and began running towards the pathway through the bushes that had lead them to the mound.

One man wasn't so lucky when the creature grabbed him from behind as he tried to run away.

The man swung feebly at the creature as it raised him up above its head with both arms and then hurled him at a group of men trying to make their way through the passage.

The man landed on two of the other men and caused them to fall forward as they were attempting to run away.

The beast pounced was on them instantly and began pounding them with its fist.

Rowan ran through the bush pathway with Hakon closely behind.  They continued to run with the rest of the other men as fast as they could down the hill.

Glancing back, Rowan could see the creature fighting one of the men that had been knocked down. The man who'd been thrown wasn't moving and the other man was scrambling to get up and run away.

The draug began beating the other man to death while the rest of the men continued to run down the hill.

The other man who had managed to get up and started to run. He still had his bow and after he'd ran a few feet away, he turned and carefully aimed an arrow at the creature.

It was a solid shot and the arrow hit the beast in the eye.

The draug roared the most hideous bone-chilling howl anyone had ever heard in their lives. It was so laud that Rowan was sure the village could hear it too.

The creature grabbed the arrow stuck in its eye and began trying to pull it out. It acted different than it had when it hit by Sven's arrows. When the creature was hit by Sven's arrows, it ignored them. The arrows fired by the bowman seemed to really bother the monster and cause it great pain.

He fired another arrow into the creature with such accuracy that he actually managed to hit the creature in the hand that it was using to pull the other arrow out and pin it to its face.

It was an incredible shot and caused the beast to let out an ear piercing howl louder than before.

Both Rowan and Hakon momentarily stopped running to look in amazement.

The creature was now extremely angry. With a
ferocious roar it ripped its hand free and snapped off
the arrow shafts, leaving the arrow heads embedded
in its head.

Seeing the creature injured, everyone who'd been
fleeing had briefly stopped tp turn back and fight.
However that notion was quickly thrown away
when they saw the beast roar again and took a great
leap towards the archer.

The beast landed directly on him and crushed
him mercilessly.

Witnessing the impossible strength and speed of
the creature, and its ability to leap great distances,
everyone simultaneously turned and began running
again.

And run they did.

The remaining men ran down the hill with all
their speed. One injured man even threw his shield
and ax to the ground to help him run faster.

Not one them bothered looking back.

It was all they could do. They had already lost
most of the men immediately upon meeting this
creature and it was clear that they would not be able
to take it down.

It was better to run and live to fight another day.

They continued to run as long as they could until exhaustion took over and they stopped running to rest for a moment.  They had all looked back and carefully listened to see if the creature gave chase. It had been a few minutes since they heard its howling in the distance.

"I don't see it," said Hakon as he tried to catch his breath.

"Its not chasing us," said Rowan.

"How do you know that?"

"It's faster than us."

Hakon gave him a nervous nod.

They gathered together to catch their breath and see who had survived.

"There are only four of us left," said Hakon. "Five armed veteran men had fallen and I don't even think we really even hurt it."

Everyone nodded in agreement.

"Did you see how it acted when the arrows hit it?"

"Yes," said a man, "it was hurt when we fought it by its mound."

"I saw that," said Hakon, "but it didn't slow it any."

"Do you think we should try again?"

"No," said Hakon, "there is no way we can defeat it like this. We need to return and notify the Jarl what has happened."

Rowan had mixed feelings. He glad that he was no longer accused of and going be executed for murder, but his future was still in question.

There was still the fact that they'd lost over half the expedition and had ran away. It was considered a cowardly act to run away from any battle, win or lose.

The four defeated men gathered themselves and made one final look back to make sure the draug wasn't coming for them. Once satisfied that they weren't being pursued, they made their way back through the forest towards the village.

# Chapter 8

The expedition's survivors made their way back to the village. Word quickly passed of their arrival and many of the men in the village dropped what they were doing to gather in the Jarl's Hall to find out what had happened.

Only four souls of the nine that had left managed to return. This had everyone's attention and curiosity.

It was close to dusk and there were already men gathered in the Hall who'd been anxiously awaiting the return of the expedition.

The four defeated men quietly stepped into the jarl's hall. Everyone went silent as they walked past them and made their way to the jarl, who sat talking with Alvis the lawspeaker.

Rowan gathered the strangest looks being he was carrying Bjord's ax and wasn't bound in chains.

Jarl Erling got up from his chair and met them halfway.

"What happened," he asked. "Where are the rest of the men I sent with you?"

"Lord," Hakon said, "all that the thrall Rowan had told us was the truth."

Many of the men in the hall immediately demanded to know what had happened and why the thrall dare enter the jarl's hall armed with an ax.

"Silence!" shouted the jarl.

Everyone in the hall hushed quiet.

"Tell me everything that has happened," he said, "were you attacked?"

"My lord," Hakon said, "we met the creature at the mound and I regret to inform you that we were defeated in battle by it. My lord, the other men have fallen."

"Fallen? How could this have happened?"

"My lord, we left this morning as planned. The thrall showed us the trail where the blacksmith's sheep had ran into the forest. We followed the trail through the woods and up the hillside for a distance and found the remains of two different sheep along the way."

130

"Remains?  What happened to them?"

"My lord, it appears that wild animals had eaten most of the sheep's corpses. The thrall informed us that the sheep were dead when he first followed the trail with the blacksmith and his son."

"I understand," he said, "continue."

"The thrall then led us to the location where he claimed that he escaped the creature that killed his master and his son."

"Were there any signs of Bjord or his son," asked the jarl. "Did you find their bodies?"

"My lord, there was a passageway torn through some bushes which led to what looked like a hidden burial mound. The bodies of Bjord the blacksmith and his son were there."

"Were you able to tell how they were killed? Were they murdered?"

"My lord, the bodies were mutilated by something that was not a man."

"Not a man?  What do you mean?"

"My lord, we were met by the very creature that the thrall had said killed the blacksmith and his son."

The men listening in hall began talking loudly amongst themselves. They questioned the very existence of such a thing and a few men even mocked the notion and laughed the very moment they heard it.

Jarl Erling walked back to his chair and sat down, taking it all in for a moment.

"Silence!" yelled Jarl Erling as he stood back up. "I demand that this hall remain quiet while I am trying to talk to the caption of my own housekarl guard! I will clear this hall by force to quieted it if I must!"

The members of his housekarl guard present immediately stepped forward at the ready of his command.

The hall quietened and the jarl waved his guards to stand down.

He sat back down and then calmly looked at Hakon and said, "continue."

"Yes my lord," he said, "the creature, or rather the draug I believe it is called, was a huge beast. It was bigger than a man and even bigger than a bear."

"Oh, now we're going to hear epic sagas about slaying dragons and giants," said a man in the hall as he laughed, even though nobody laughed with him.

Jarl Erling shot him a quick look and then nodded at Hakon to continue.

"It had dead looking eyes and its flesh seemed to be rotting because the smell was horrendous."

"I have never heard of such a thing," said the jarl, "are you sure?"

"My lord Erling," said Alvis the lawspeaker, "your captain's description is how I heard the elders describe them of my day. It is a draug. The thrall's tale of a cat coming to him in the night and trying to kill him is also said of them. It is said that they can change their shape into such things."

The Jarl thought about this.

"Were your men able to slay the creature," he asked, "this 'draug'?"

"My lord," said Hakon, "the beast was too powerful. It was on us as fast as lightning and it was as powerful as charging bull, maybe stronger. We were unable to inflict any damage to it and were lucky to escape it."

"You weren't able to harm it in any way?" asked Jarl Erling. "There must be a way to slay this abomination."

Rowan looked up at the jarl as if he wanted to say something, but remained quiet. Jarl Erling noticed and spoke directly at him.

"Speak thrall," he said, "you may speak freely."

"My lord," said Rowan, "I think their weapons burned it when they hit it."

"Burned it?"

"My lord," said Alvis, "ancient lore tells us that most of the unseen creatures in the forest can be harmed only with weapons made of iron.  Perhaps the iron made weapons may be the key to destroying this draug."

"Yes, I have to agree." Hakon said. "One of the bowmen hit the beast with arrows that had sharp iron tips.  When they embedded into the creature, it appeared to hurt it."

"Yes my lord," Rowan said, "I remember the creature struggled violently to get my master's ax out of its back. It was when I seized the moment to escape."

Jarl Erling stood up and addressed the men in the hall.

"Men, our village is plagued by a creature with the blood of many men on its hands.  We must find a way to destroy this thing and rid ourselves of its curse before any more men from this village die."

Gwenda and her mother Helga appeared at the hall's door and entered just as Jarl Erling made this announcement.

"My lord," said Gwenda, "what has been discovered about the fate of my son and husband?"

She knew in her heart that Rowan's story was true. She had witnessed the hellish cat chasing the livestock with her own eyes. But in her heart, she hoped that they would find her husband and son merely lost or injured and return them to her.

"Please," said Jarl Erling, "come sit."

He motioned for one of his thralls to fetch both the blacksmith's widow and her mother a chair to be seat before him.

Gwenda and Helga made their way to the seats provided and quietly sat down. She kept her gaze on the jarl and patiently waited for him to deliver the news she knew she did not want to hear.

"Madam," said the jarl, "dear widow of the blacksmith, I have dire news. We have confirmed the thrall's story to have been the truth. Your husband and son are dead. I am sorry."

Gwenda sank in her chair and began to weep while Helga tried to comfort her. They had already been mentally prepared to hear the bad news, but no amount of preparation can ready anyone to actually hear it being said. She has lost her husband and also her only son. All the men of her household have perished. What was to become of them.

She still had the thrall, but he was unfortunately not trained in the art of blacksmithing. This had been their livelihood for generations. This was a disaster to her family.

Jarl Erling tried to offer her comfort and took the ax from Rowan and handed it to her.

"Rest assured madam," he said, "we will destroy the creature that killed your husband and son. Here is your husband's ax that was recovered."

"Thank you my lord," said Gwenda, "but that won't replace him or our livelihood. Our thrall is now the only male of the household and he is not trained as a blacksmith."

Overhearing her say this, Oleg, the karl that had discovered Rowan walked over.

"I am truly sorry for the lost of your husband and of your son," he said, "but I have made a claim for finding the thrall when he was wandering outside of the village without a master."

She was flabbergasted.

She couldn't believe after all that has happened, that this man had the gall to make such a claim against her household and at a time like this.

She angrily stood up and said, "how dare you make a claim of property upon the death of my husband and against my household!"

"I mean no disrespect," said Oleg, "with the men of the household gone, the thrall is now without a legal owner and he is not a freed man.  Ownership is to whoever first claims him."

"My husband's property belongs to his household which passes to me now by marital right!"

Seeing their argument beginning to heat up, Jarl Erling called upon the lawspeaker to make a legal decision on the matter.

"Lawspeaker," he said, "please recite the law of our people on this matter so we may put this dispute to rest."

Alvis the law-speaker stood up and spoke loud enough for all in the hall to hear.

"It has been the custom of our people for many generations before I walked this earth that when the father dies, the father's property fell upon to that of the first born son.  If the first born was already dead, then it went to the next born son and so forth."

"The blacksmith Bjord and his son have been killed," Oleg said, "this leaves no other heirs or sons to claim the property because a wife does not inherit her husband's property."

"Then the property would pass to the man's male

family," said Thorn, "this would make the thrall and the remaining property owned by my brother Bjord now my property because I was his brother and his only remaining male blood kin."

"This is not true in this case," said the lawspeaker.

"How can that be so," said Thorn, "when they both died?"

"Because the property never was his in the first place," said Alvis, "it belonged to Gwenda."

"That is nonsense!" said Thorn.

"The property belonged to Gwenda before she married Bjord," he said. "She had been gifted it by her father when she gave birth to her son from her first marriage."

"In accordance to the law as has been recited by the lawspeaker," Jarl Erling said, "the thrall and all property belongs to and will be returned to Gwenda. This is the law of our people and there will be no further arguments."

Oleg sat down hard on a bench. He was disappointed, but accepted the ruling.  He had no choice, to go against the law as recited by the lawspeaker and decreed by the jarl would make him a criminal.

Thorn, who'd hoped to gain a thrall and all of his brother Bjord's property, stormed out of the hall without any further word.

'Woman," said the jarl, "take claim of your thrall."

"Thank you, my lord."

Gwenda, assisting her mother, left the jarl's hall with an uncertain Rowan following behind them.

Rowan wasn't sure of what had all just taken place.  Everything seemed to have gone by so very quickly in so many extremes.  Nevertheless, he was glad to be out of the jarl's hall and alive.  He was no longer being accused of murder and he was no longer facing an almost certain horrible death by execution.

# Chapter 9

For the first time in days, Rowan laid in familiar bedding. It essentially was nothing more than a sack made from scrap cloth stuffed with straw with an old worn deer hide which laid over it. But all things considered over the past few days, it felt like the most comfortable bed in the world to Rowan.

He laid there lost in thought as he stared out the open door into the curtain of darkness outside. It was a humid sticky night and they'd left the door open to let the cooler breeze of the night air come in.

It was relaxing to hear the nocturnal creatures at night go about their nightly routines with the smell of the fresh night breeze cleansing the stale air inside the longhouse.

His thoughts raced through the events that had happened over the past few days. Quite a bit took place. Life changing events that had forever changed how things would be from now on.

Not only was the household of which he belonged permanently changed with a now uncertain future, but the line that divided what was real and what was fantasy was also now blurred and distorted.

As Rowan stared outside he noticed a small pair of eyes looking back at him from just outside the door in the darkness.

He was instantly alarmed by it and hastily sat up.

Rowan was afraid that perhaps the draug had returned in some other form. Like it did when it showed up shape shifted as a cat. It could also be some other creature with ill intent. He had no way of really knowing. He only knew that now he trusted nothing.

Rowan reached for a small ax that was setting on the table while still peering outside at the eyes cloaked in the darkness. The reflection in the eyes did not seem to be like those of a critter, although by their size and proximity to the ground it had to be a small creature.

Armed with the ax, Rowan gingerly approached the door. He didn't want to wake anyone else up in the house, in case it was just a woodland creature or some other harmless critter looking to nip some food.

As he got closer to it, there was a degree of familiarity about it. Yes, the eyes in the darkness were familiar to him.  Indeed the eyes were not those belonging to a hare, lynx, or even a fox.

As soon as he stepped outside the door, he heard it say, "come over here."

Her recognized the voice instantly.  It was Tom Taye, that unusual creature that was in the hollow with him.

Rowan was unsure about this Tom character, but he did save him from being discovered by the troll and he did lead him in the right direction to get back to his village.

Tom noticed Rowan's hesitation as he stood in the doorway.

"It's okay," Tom said, "come on out. I don't want to disturb anyone in the house. We need to talk."

At this point curiosity was what finally pushed Rowan out the door. He walked outside and could see the outline of Tom hiding in the shadows.  From what he could make out, Tom looked like a very, very small man.  No taller than a house cat or hare. This was very strange and made Rowan extremely nervous.  He'd never seen or heard of a man being so small.  What kind a queer folk was Tom?

"Why do you hide yourself?" asked Rowan.

"I don't think you're ready to gaze upon me just yet," said Tom. "The sight of me may frighten you and that is not my intent."

"I don't think I would be frightened," said Rowan. "Especially after all of the things that I've seen recently."

"Ah yes," he said, "your problem with the draug. That is why I have called upon you this very night."

"What do you mean?"

"It will come back," Tom said, "it seeks restitution and it will keep coming until it feels satisfied."

"I don't understand."

"This creature will keep returning to cause havoc and death to not only your people but to everything else unless it is put to rest," Tom said. "It is an unnatural abomination that needs to be put to rest and I think you are just the person to do it."

"Oh no," said Rowan, "I barely escaped with my life every time I dealt with that creature. And it was nothing short of pure luck that I survived each time, I might add."

"Yes, but that is only because you went about it all wrong. There is something you don't know about it. That creature, like many unseen beings, has a great weakness."

"What do you mean," asked Rowan, "are you like the draug?"

"No, not even close. But there is something about it that we do share in common and that is a great weakness to iron."

"Iron?" said Rowan. "Why iron?"

"It's a very long story as to why," Tom said, "but do know that iron burns us. We can't stand it. It has something to with its unnaturalness. Even the scent of it is foul to me and my kind.  It is foul to me now as I speak to you near it."

"But, didn't the draug enter this longhouse when it tried to kill me and then ran off the sheep?"

"Yes, that was very unusual. It must have been very determined to enter. Or maybe because it was in the form of a cat, I don't know. At first I thought it might be as immune to iron as mankind is, but then I saw that it was hurt by iron."

"What?"

"When you stuck the ax into it. It wasn't the ax blow that hurt it but the iron embedded in its flesh that did. The ax's iron head burned it as did the arrows that had iron tips on them."

"I did notice that," Rowan said, "but I wasn't sure what caused it. The iron seemed to burn it as if it was red hot from the forge."

"Yes and that is how you will be able to defeat it."

"Defeat it? Like I said, I barely escaped with my life ...twice. There is no way I intend to face it again. That beast killed trained warriors, some of the jarl's best men and they were armed with iron weapons as well."

"You are right," Tom said, "you won't be able to defeat it directly in combat. It is too strong."

"I have no plans on battling or defeating it," said Rowan. "My plan is to never go into the cursed forest ever again.  I plan to avoid it the best as I can."

"You don't have any choice, Rowan. That creature has its mind set on killing everyone in this village. It won't stop until it kills each and everyone of you. Especially you.  It seeks vengeance on you. You have to put an end to it, before it ends you."

"Why, what did I do to it?" Rowan gasped, "I'm just a thrall."

"Not true," said Tom, "you have a destiny that you do not even know of yet. You do not know who you are or where you come from. You were not just a discovered orphan that was placed into servitude as a thrall. You were made as a thrall to hide you and your identity until the time had come for you to know who you are."

Rowan laughed at this notion.

"I do not believe you.  I have always been just a thrall."

"Do you remember coming to this land from across the sea?" Tom asked.

"I do know that I am not from here, but I do not know where it was that I had came from."

"You came here by sea, yes?"

Rowan nodded.

"You were transported in a merchant's knarr ship by a trader that had found you. But the trader who brought you and sold you to the blacksmith was no ordinary trader. He was in disguise."

"What do you mean?" said Rowan in disbelief.

"He was to bring you to a safe place and hide you from those who sought an end to your bloodline. He couldn't hide you himself for fear of being discovered. So he hide you in these lands disguised as a thrall."

"I have never heard such a thing," said Rowan. "I think you may be mistaken."

"By not letting you know who you really were was the best way to keep your true identity a secret. Not even the blacksmith knew.  When he purchased you to be his thrall, he swore an oath to sell you back for double the price without any to the trader when he came back for you years later.  He also swore an oath to tell no one of this promise that he made to the trader."

Rowan stood quietly for a moment taking all this in. He remembered a night when the blacksmith was drunk and told Rowan that he was only temporarily his thrall.  He had no idea what Bjord meant by that and just assumed it was 'drunk talk'. Nevertheless the statement had stuck with him.

"So who am I?" asked Rowan.

"That is not important right now," Tom said. "What is important, is...."

"What do you mean it isn't important right now?" Rowan said. "Then why did you tell me such things?"

"It is not important right now, because it is not your time to know yet," said Tom. "And it is not your time to die yet either. The only way to stop your death is if you slay the creature before it comes back."

"How do you know its even coming back?"

"Because I have saw the creature come to the edge of the woods near here and look upon this very village.  It has been seeking restitution and will not rest in its grave until it gets it. Everyone here in this village is in mortal danger because of it."

"What can we do to stop it from coming?"

"I have a plan that might work," said Tom. "It won't stop it, but it may slow it down enough."

"Slow it down?"

"Yes, slow it down," said Tom shrugging off Rowan's question. "The iron not only hurts the creature, but also weakens it. You can use the creature's weakness against it."

"How so?" asked Rowan.

"I think you can use the blacksmith's scraps of iron within this longhouse and make a trap."

Rowan laughed.

"How would I possibly make a trap with scraps of iron?"

"You must use your imagination and think!"

Rowan could sense the annoyance in Tom's voice but he didn't really care. He wasn't going to go get himself killed.

"You're crazy if you think I'm going to risk my

neck again going anywhere near that creature."

In the distance they heard a faint howling in the darkness.

"It is angry and will not stop," Tom said, "You have no choice."

"Okay, you've convinced me. But you said you had a plan. You must understand, I have never trapped anything before. I am not a hunter. You said you had a plan, what is your plan?"

"Find a net and string bits of iron all through it. Then make a trap and lure the draug into it," explained Tom. "Once you have the draug under the net with iron, drop it and it will be trapped under the iron long enough for you to attack it."

"Wait a minute, how am I to do all of this anyways? The lady of the house, my mistress Gwenda, will never allow me to leave nor will she allow me to take any iron. She plans to sell it all to traders."

"Traders? Does she plan to trade it all tomorrow?"

"No, they plan to trade wool and other items tomorrow.  I'm suppose to take care of the livestock and gather iron for her while they're away. I believe she plans to trade it soon. There is no way I'll have time to do all of that and the task you ask of me."

"Don't worry about any of that," Tom said. "I will come in tomorrow after you leave and take care of everything in the household. You focus on the task at hand."

Rowan heard something topple to ground behind him somewhere in the blacksmithing area.

He turned and looked around, nervous that it may be that cat again.

"Probably that stupid goat," he said as he turned back around, but Tom was gone.

Rowan looked around, but couldn't see very well in the darkness and decided that Tom wasn't coming back.  He went back inside to look around to make that noise was just the goat, but Grumpy was no where to be found.

Rowan was too tired to care.  He needed his rest for the next day's tasks at hand and went back to bed.  Nervously looking around the longhouse periodically until he finally drifted off.

# Chapter 10

In the morning after the women of the house had left for the day, Rowan began getting ready. It would be his only chance to do this because they planned to be gone the entire day in the village center to trade.

Many knarrs with traders were expected to show up and Gwenda had hopes that she'd be able to trade wool and other goods. They planned to trade the blacksmithing items and scrap iron tomorrow.

Nobody else would be in the longhouse today, so Rowan took his chance to set his plan into action. Gwenda had tasked him to take care of the livestock and clean up her late husband's blacksmithing items to be traded.

Tom had promised Rowan that he would take care of everything that needed to be done when Rowan was away. Excluding the iron blacksmith items of course.

Tom said he'd show up after Rowan left to deal with the draug.  Rowan had no choice but to hope Tom kept his word and showed up.  For now, he had to get busy if he had any hopes of completing the dreadful task that laid ahead.

Rowan gathered up as much iron items as he could. Iron scraps, pieces of slag, pig iron, whatever he could find. There were two unfinished shirts of chain mail that Bjord had been working on. Rowan grabbed those as well.  He figured that he could use them to help trap the beast.

He had two wooden buckets full of assorted scrap iron, a sling with several ax heads strung on it, and two partial shirts of chain mail rolled in a bundle across his back.  He also grabbed the fishing net that was hanging in the rafters, along with some twine and rope.

He had quite a load to carry and he was already struggling with it. He had to drop some of the iron if he was going to be able to carry it through the forest.

He decided to divide the weight on a yoke which he put over his shoulder to help bear the weight through the forest and up the hillside.

Rowan tied as much as he could to the shoulder pole, including Bjord's ax which Gwenda had set next to his anvil.  He lifted the heavy load up on his shoulder. It was heavy, but not as bad as he thought it would be. He dropped a couple more ax heads to lighten the load a bit more and headed out the door.

Taking one last look behind him at the longhouse, he made his was through the forest and up the hill towards the draug's burial mound.

Rowan's mind drifted here and there as he made the walk. This was his third time taking this path and he no longer needed to track it. Unfortunately, he now knew the way by heart.

There were some serious doubts in his thinking as to whether or not he'd be successful doing this. He tried to think of ways to make his plan work out, but most of his thoughts wandered on the fact that he felt this was his last trip to the creature's mound.

Not because he felt he would successfully trap and kill it, but because he felt his best efforts would be futile and the draug was certain to kill him.

By time he made it to the area just before where the draug's mound was located, he was already tired and covered in sweat from bearing the load. He'd been keeping a steady pace with only short rests. But he only stopped to rest long enough to catch his breath.

He wanted to get up to the location while there was still plenty of daylight to work in.

Looking around at the pathway through the bushes, he could smell the creature's foul scent of death and knew it was close.

He tried to keep quiet and not attract its attention, even though he didn't think it mattered because the creature probably could sense him anyways. It had the knack of simply just showing up.

Most of all, he tried not to look at the bodies of the brave men who had taken him up there to prove his story about the creature in the first place. Their bodies laid where they had fallen and seeing their mangled corpses didn't help Rowan's confidence in the slightest bit.

This was a place of death begat by death.

Trying to stay focused, Rowan set down his load and set to work as quickly as he could. He had to quickly make the trap if he had any hope of successfully pulling it off.

That is, if his plan would even work at all.

Casting these negative thoughts to the wind, he began to make the snare. Initially, he was going to dig a pit and make a dead fall for the creature, but in his haste to gather iron he forgot to bring a shovel.

He could use his the ax and his hands, but it

would still take too much time to prepare and the creature would probably show up before he got the hole dug anyways.

Thinking better, he decided to make a snare to trip the creature or at least slow it down enough so he could get the net over it ...somehow.

Rowans laid out the fishing net. It wasn't as big as he wanted it to be, but it would do. He used the twine he brought to tie bits of iron to the netting. The idea was when the net was over the creature, the scattered iron pieces tied in would be pressing on it at multiple locations.

He took the rope he had and cut several lengths. With the rope lengths he tied knots and between each knot he threaded an ax head.

Once he got the net over the creature, he figured he could wrap the rope around it and bind it with the iron ax heads pressing against it and further disabling it.

He hung the net from some tree limbs above and tied knots holding the net to limbs. He tied it so he could pull them loose with a tug from a single length of rope. He tied the net up a couple times and pulled the rope loose to make sure it would work as he planned. After a few tries, he got it to drop exactly how he wanted it to.

At the spot where the net dropped, he laid the chain mail shirts down and tied them together with twine. He laid them so they would lay flat and wide. He threaded rope through blanket of chain mail and tossed the rope ends over a strong limb above.

He bent a young tree down and tied it down to a tree root sticking out of the ground. Then he tied the rope leading to the chain mail to the bent over tree.

Now all he had to do was cut the rope holding the bent over tree.

His plan was that the tree would spring back up and pull the chain mail up tight around the beast's legs.  He concealed the chain mail with leaves so the draug wouldn't see it. And also so the iron wouldn't burn its feet and expose the trap.

He set Bjord's ax down by the tied off rope so it would be at the ready.

According to plan, he'd lure the creature into the spot and pull the rope so the net dropped down on it.  Once the net dropped, he'd cut the rope holding the tree down so it would pull the chain mail up over its legs.  Then all he had to do after that was grab the rope with the iron ax heads threaded through it and wrap it around the beast while it was snared.

The rest of his plan relied on using Bjord's ax to

finish the creature off.

Now, all he had to do was lure the creature into the spot.  This, he had not worked out yet.

Plan B entailed running away as fast as he could. But in all truth, there was no plan B.  He'd never be able to outrun the creature and he knew it wouldn't let him escape again.

This had to work.

# Chapter 11

A couple hours had passed since Rowan had finished making his trap.  He'd been sitting on the ground holding the rope to the net and watching the passageway to the draug's burial mound.

Quietly watching and waiting for it to come on its own.

He hoped that he could safely wait there and the draug would just come from, well wherever it came from by the mound, and just head towards him so he could trap it.  But that obviously wasn't going to happen.  He was going to have to expose himself and lure the creature to the trap.

Rowan didn't like this idea.

This was where things got tricky because there was a great chance he'd never get the creature to the trap and an even greater chance the creature would kill him before he even had the chance to trap it.

This was why he waited in this spot with the trap between him and the passageway.  It was the safest way with the best chance to get the creature in the exact spot he needed it to be.

Unfortunately, the safest way was not going to work.  He had no choice but to try and lure it in.

Reluctantly, Rowan got up from the ground and grabbed the ax he'd set up to cut the snare line and started walking towards the passageway to the beast's mound.

Already he could feel his heart pounding from both anticipation and fear.

He walked through the passageway taking slow steps without taking his eyes off the mound.  When he got to the other side, he stood there and tried to come up with a way he could lure the beast out. He needed to bring it out into the open and then get it to chase him to the trap...without getting killed.

There was no real way to do it safely. It was all or nothing.

Before he could talk himself out of it, Rowan abruptly walked right up to the burial mound and kicked some of the rocks loose.

He then turned around and quickly ran to the opening in the pathway and looked behind him.

He held the ax at the ready, expecting the creature to suddenly show up, literally anywhere. He carefully looked around looked in every direction for even the slightest movement.

Nothing.

This time he walked over and stood on the mound while kicked more rocks off of it. He hoped this would disturb and bring it out. Rowan knew it was in there somewhere. That was where it came out from when it formed from a mist. Both times it had come out of the mound in a mist.

Rowan stood on the mound for a few minutes, turning and looking in every direction. He watched for the beast or any sign of the mist to coming up.

There was still nothing.

This wasn't going to plan in any shape or form. He simply wasn't going to be able to lure the beast out of its mound this way.

A huge part of him was glad for that.

This wasn't going to work, despite him showing up and carrying out the plan with a mockery of bravery that really didn't exist in him. It was more in desperation that led him to carry out this plan. That and Tom, a creature he wasn't even sure about, convincing him that he could do it.

There was only a few hours of daylight left and Rowan knew that it would be best to gather the iron back up and carry it back down before his mistress Gwenda came back home.

Being that he wasn't successful in getting himself killed with this hair-brained plan, he may as well not get in trouble for taking the iron and going into the forest as well. He'd not been given permission to do this.

Rowan started walking back to dismantle his trap and gather everything up, but as he started walking through the passage, he noticed the tell-tale mist forming from the creature.

*"Here it comes!" he thought.*

His heart sank. He'd already accepted and was grateful that the creature didn't show up.

Now it was coming.

Rowan slowly turned around and looked towards the mound.  There it stood. The grotesquely bloated creature the elders called a draug.

It formed in the mist when Rowan had his back turned and was walking back towards the trap. It probably sought to ambush him.

Rowan looked directly at it as it looked right back at him.

*"This was a VERY bad idea."*

Rowan immediately darted off at full speed towards his trap.  If he could get to the rope before it reached the drop spot, he'd have a chance to trap it.  It was the only chance he had.  He knew he'd never outrun it and escape.

It had to be trapped otherwise he was now trapped.

Rowan ran with everything he had.  He could hear the beast angrily howl and its footsteps pounding the ground behind him.

The chase was on.

He got past the passageway and was heading to the rope.  He had to get to it.  Rowan never ran so fast in his life. He was in sheer panic and almost dropped the ax.

He was going to make it!

Just as he stepped over the chain mail he'd hidden under the leaves, his foot caught a piece of rope and he tripped.

Rowan tumbled face first over his trap and dropped the ax as he rolled out of control on the ground.

He quickly got up and looked for the ax.

It was on the ground next to the chain mail snare trap.  He ran to grab it and saw that the beast was almost on him.

Rowan picked up the ax and turned to go cut the rope.  As soon as he stood back, the creature swung at him and barely missed his head as it drove its monstrosity of a fist into the ground.

Rowan swung the ax and hit it in the leg. He cut deeply into it and the creature roared in anger. Rowan turned towards the rope and swung his ax to cut the rope and snare the beast.

The ax bounced off the rope when he swung down on it.

He swung again and it bounced off again. He glimpsed at the creature and saw that it was still in the trap spot. Rowan quickly reached over and pulled the other rope and released the iron laced fisherman's net down on top of the creature.

The net dropped as planned, but did not land completely covering the creature as he wanted.  Part of the net fell to the side and hung over the creature's head and shoulder, only covering half of its body.

The iron trick was working and the beast howled furiously in pain. The bits of iron that were in the net laid on its flesh and burned it.

166

The creature swung around madly as it tried to get the net off.  Rowan noticed that it was now standing with both feet directly over the chain mail snare and he tried to cut the rope again.

He swung down on the rope and the ax bounced off it again. It only cut a few threads of the rope.

Frustrated, Rowan took a step forward and swung the ax at the root where he tied it down.  This time it cut through and released the snare.

The  bent over tree sprung back up and pulled the chain mail up and around the creature's feet and legs.

It screeched in a furious madness as the chain mail wrapped around its lower body. The iron burned it wherever it touched the creature's cursed dead flesh.

Remembering the rope strung with iron ax heads, Rowan dropped the ax and quickly ran over to picked it up from the ground. He threw the rope around the beast as it was trying to get itself lose from the netting and managed to get it around it legs. He then ran around the creature while holding the rope as it roared at him.  He wrapped the rope around the beast several times and then pulled at it.

He was trying to knock the creature over but the forsaken thing was too heavy and stood firm.

It was like trying to pull an oak tree down, so Rowan ran around to the other side and picked up the ax.

Just as Rowan picked the ax up from the ground, the creature managed to get an arm loose and swung at him.

It missed and tried to step forward towards Rowan and swung at him again, but tripped over the entanglement around its legs.

The draug fell to the ground and howled as it struggled to get itself free. This was the opportunity Rowan needed. He picked up the ax with both hands and lifted it above his head. He took one last look at the creature before he brought the ax down on its head with all his might.

A dull thud announced the ax hitting its mark.

The grotesque thing dropped it arms and emitted a low growl.

Surprisingly, it was still alive. Such a direct blow to the head would have ended any living being. Yet this thing wasn't really even alive. This cursed thing shouldn't even be walking around in the first place.

With difficultly Rowan pulled the ax from the thing's head. It was so deeply embedded that he had to put his foot on the thing's back to gain leverage pull the ax free.

As soon as he pulled the ax out of the creature, it persevered struggling to get free.

There was only one way to end all of this madness and Rowan knew what he had to do. He raised the bloodied ax over his head once again. This time he aimed for the creature's neck as he swung down with all his force.

He struck the draug's unnatural swollen neck, but failed to chop its head off.

It took Rowan two more chops to separate the creature's head from its body. When he did, the abomination's body stopped moving and dropped limply to the ground.

He'd done it.

He'd actually done it.

Rowan looked down at the creature's still body as it laid there on the ground wrapped in net, chain mail, rope, and iron. Its flesh sizzling wherever the iron touched it. The smell made Rowan's stomach churn.

To Rowan's horror, he still heard growling.

He looked over to where he heard the growls and saw that the creature's head was still alive!

Rowan looked down at the head and grabbed it by the hair. He lifted it up and looked at its dead, lifeless white eyes. They were still open as was its mouth. The thing was actually trying to growl, but the only sound that came out was a drowned out gurgling sound.

It repulsed him so he tossed it back on the ground as it snared and bite wildly into the air. He rolled it over with his foot so that its face was towards the ground.

He stood back and looked at the thing's body again.

It was over, but the burden of his dirty work was not yet complete. There was simply too much risk of this thing coming back again.  The only way to make sure it was dead and stayed dead was to burn it.

Rowan began gathering dead wood around the area and started stacking the firewood on top of the creature's corpse. He was going to make a bonfire and burn it.

At first he was going to dig a hole and roll the creature in it. This way he could burn it in the hole and then easily cover the hole up. But when he tried to roll the thing's headless body over, it was too heavy and he wasn't able to budge it at all.

It was like a solid rock that would take a team of

horses to move, so he decided to burn it where it laid.

He would still need proof of killing it.

Although he was not happy about it, he really hadn't any choice. He would have carry the thing's head back to the jarl as proof of the creature's demise.

Rowan gathered the ghastly still active head with its dull gurgling growl and placed it in one of the buckets he used to carry the iron scraps up the mountain.

He went back around and gathered enough firewood to make a big enough fire to burn the creature's body to ash.  Once he'd set the hastily built funeral pyre on fire, he sat back and watched the smoke from the fire roll into the sky for a couple hours. He watched the fire until he was satisfied that the corpse was going to be reduced to ash.

He had to make sure that it would never rise again.

It was getting late and the Sun was ready to set. Rowan made a torch and lit it from the bonfire's blaze. He gathered his things, including the bucket with the moaning head in it, and made his way down the mountainside towards the village.

# Chapter 12

Rowan arrived at the village's edge just a little after night fall. Once again he found himself standing at the wood's edge trying to decide what to do.  It was either go to the longhouse of his mistress and wait until morning; or to continue on and go to the jarl's hall and report slaying the beast now.

One thing was for certain, he needed to take a short break because he was exhausted. Even though he killed the creature, he didn't want to be in the mountain's forest at night and when he set out he didn't stop and kept steadfast.

The now defeated creature wasn't the only threat that lurked within the forest.  Rowan had come to learn there were many things in the wilderness that were more of a threat than wolves and bears.

Thankful of the moonlight that lit the way, he set his bundle down and looked around.

The moonlight helped him find his way through the last stretch of forest.  His torch had burned itself out already and he didn't bother to make another. Once he got out of the thick of the forest, he was somewhat able to see without using a torch.

Feeling rested enough from his short 'breather', Rowan gathered up his things and made his way towards the jarl's hall. He knew the jarl and a majority of the men of the village would the there. There simply was no better time to do this than now.

If he went back to the longhouse, Gwenda would surely be angry because he had left without permission. And he'd taken the chain mail and iron.

It wasn't long until Rowan was standing just outside the jarl's hall.  He could hear the muffled voices of the men inside and set everything he was carrying down by the outside wall.

He picked up the bucket containing the head and Bjord's ax. He walked up to the doorway and stood there a moment. He could still hear the creature's muffled groans inside the bucket. It was strange how its body-less head was still alive.

Rowan was still hesitant to just walk inside.  He was just a thrall and he wasn't exactly permitted to enter without a master or without a really good reason.

174

"Silly thought. This was reason enough," he reassured himself as gathering the courage to enter.

As soon as he stepped foot in the hall, his presence was immediately noticed by men near the door. One of them was about to confront him until another man standing next to him saw what Rowan was carrying and stopped him.

A housekarl standing by the door also saw what Rowan was carrying and called out loud enough to be heard above the other conversing voices and merriment in the jarl's hall.

"My lord!"

The hall quickly went quiet as everyone turned and looked at Rowan. The guard motioned him to go to the jarl and followed behind him as he walked.

Men stepped out of his way as he walked towards the jarl. Some gasped as they saw what was in the bucket Rowan carried as he passed them.

With a degree of uneasiness Rowan walked past all the gawking men, who at first looked upon him with disgust until they saw what he was carrying inside of his bucket.

He made his way past everyone and stood before the Jarl, who was sitting in his throne looking at him with a curious look on his face.

Rowan tried to keep his eyes lowered. He didn't want to provoke anyone's wrath upon him, especially that of the jarl.

As soon as he got in front of the jarl, he set the bucket down before the Jarl Erling's feet and took a step back before he kneeling down on one knee.

"My lord, I present to you the draug's head."

The men in the hall erupted in an almost instant roar as soon as they heard Rowan announce this. Some of the voices were of cheering, while others were of those expressing their doubts.

Jarl Erling leaned forward in his chair and looked down into the bucket. He was immediately revolted when he saw the creature's head.

Even though the jarl was a seasoned warrior, he still didn't like the sight of blood or dead things. But he was the leader and he couldn't show even an ounce of weakness, no matter how much the thing repulsed him. He needed to verify the thrall's claim.

He leaned forward and reached down into the bucket and flipped the head over so he could see its face. As soon as he flipped it over, he quickly pulled his hand back and stood up.

The hall got quiet.

Jarl Erling looked down at Rowan and then

turned his gaze to the other men in the hall and said, "The beast has been slain!"

The men in the hall erupted in cheers.

The jarl sat back down and looked at Rowan.

"The head," he said,"it is still alive?"

Rowan nodded.

"Is the body still alive too?"

"No my lord, the body died when I chopped its head off," said Rowan as he handed Bjord's ax to the jarl. "The head somehow remains alive."

There was gasping by the men who peered over to look at the head in the bucket.  Rowan could hear some of them talk behind him. Many of the men in the room argued whether it was the creature's head or not.  There were many men trying to step forward and look over the heads of the other men to see for themselves.

The Jarl called over one of his guards.

"Quickly," he said, "fetch the lawspeaker."

The guard nodded and immediately made his way through the crowd before disappearing out of the hall's door.

Seeing how the men inside of the hall were crowding over each other trying to see the creature's head, Jarl Erling stood up and addressed them.

"Calm down men," said the jarl. "There is no need to crowd each other."

He reached down into the bucket, being careful not to let the thing bite him, and pulled the head up out of the bucket for all to see.

Unfortunately, as soon as he picked it up, it slipped from his grip and fell back into the bucket. It made a squishy sound when it landed which made the jarl nearly gag. The nasty rotting thing repulsed him, but again he kept it hidden from his men.

Rowan noticed the jarl's distaste at touching it and offered to take it out of the bucket.

"My lord, there is no need for you to dirty your hands touching this repulsive and vile thing," he said. "Please allow me."

The Jarl nodded and sat back down.

"Place it on the floor so all may see it," he said.

Rowan nodded and carefully reached into the bucket and picked up the creature's head. He had to hold it by its ears so it wouldn't slip out of his hands. Rowan lifted the head up and turned to face the men in the hall.

He held it up high so everyone in the hall could get a good look at it before he set the head down on the ground.

He made sure the head was upright and facing towards everyone in the hall so they could get a good look at it if they wanted.

He wiped his hands on his tunic and backed away from the head.  Rowan knelt to the side so he would still be faced the jarl, but also so he could see the head and the men in the hall.

He immediately started getting bombarded by questions. They demanded to know how he managed to kill the beast and why its head still alive, but before he could answer the jarl interrupted them.

"Men, be patient until the lawspeaker arrives and everyone shall have their questions answered," he said. "Leave the thrall be for the moment."

The creature's head was still looking around with its dead eyes and emitting the occasional growl. Although the muffled growls could barely be heard over the noise in the hall, everyone could still see its mouth move as it tried to growl and roar.

Its occasional bite at the air was the most ghastly of it all.

A large man wearing a bear skin pushed his way through the crowd to get a glimpse of the thing's head and then angrily looked at Rowan.

"How did you possibly kill it," he said. "There is no way a mere thrall could have done such a thing. Especially something so mighty that it slayed so many of our own seasoned warriors."

Rowan was about to answer the man's question, but Jarl Erling calmly lifted his hand and motioned him not to answer.

"I sent for the lawspeaker," he said. "We shall wait to hear what happened when the lawspeaker arrives and only then. I want him to hear this when we hear it so we can get his take on it all."

He looked around and could see how many of the men that were grow impatient, so he stood up and addressed the hall again.

"Please men, just be patient and enjoy the mead I have provided. Your wait for answers and to hear the thrall's story shall not be very much longer.  I sent for Alvis the Lawspeaker.  He should be here any moment."

The Jarl instructed his thralls to bring out more mead to be distributed to the men in the hall.  Many of them settled down and took in the mead. But there were others that remained disgruntled and stood impatiently waiting.

The wait for the lawspeaker wasn't very long.

He arrived at the door assisted by the housekarl that had been sent to fetch him.  The elderly man walked over and took a seat in a chair provided for him in front of the jarl.

"Welcome wise speaker of the law!" said Jarl Erling. "The head of the beast has been delivered to us."

"Are you sure?" Alvis said. "Let me see it."

"Bring the head to the lawspeaker," Jarl Erling said.

Nobody made a move.

Without looking up, Rowan stood up and walked over to the head and picked it up. He placed it in the bucket and then sat the bucket in front of Alvis the lawspeaker.

The old man leaned over and examined the gruesome head for a few minutes without saying a word as everyone looked on.  Suddenly he gasped as if he recognized its face and sat back in his chair.

This made many of the other men in the hall nervous and they started calling out different assumptions.  Some claiming that it was probably Bjord's head.

After he quietly sat for a few minutes in deep thought, he finally looked up at the jarl and nodded.

The jarl stood up and raised his hands up.

"Quiet! Men, I need the Hall to quieten."

The men in the hall began to quieten with the help of a few of the other men relaying the jarl's request.

When the hall fell silent and with everyone's attention, Jarl Erling announced,

"Now Alvis the wise, bearer of our laws, is ready to hear the thrall Rowan's testimony," he said. "The thrall named Rowan will now speak."

The Jarl sat down and motioned the now wide eyed Rowan to speak.

"Tell us Rowan," he said. "Tell us how you come to possess the head of the very creature that has slayed some of my very own men and become a plague to my jarldom."

Rowan was reluctant to speak, especially after the last time he was forced to speak before the hall when he ended up being accused of murder.

"My lord," he finally said. "The first two times that we confronted the creature we noticed that iron had hurt it.  Iron appeared to burn it, so I came up with a plan to trap it with iron."

"What compelled you to do this?" asked Alvis.

182

"I knew something had to be done about this creature," said Rowan. "It wasn't going to leave the folk of this village alone."

"What makes you think that?" blurted out a man. "Perhaps if we left it be, it would leave us be."

A few other men in the hall agreed with him.

"Because it had already killed several men already," Rowan said.

"It only killed them when they disturbed its mount," someone said. "Otherwise it didn't care about us."

"Whatever drove this creature," said the jarl. "It wasn't going to stop."

"We don't know that," said the man.

"It came after us and you can bet it was going to come back," said the jarl, "again and again."

Nobody contested this.

"Continue thrall," said the jarl, "tell us how you killed it."

"My lord, I noticed that the iron hurt the creature, so I thought I would be able to use iron to trap and kill it."

Jarl Erling nodded.

"So I gathered up a net, some rope, and as much scrap iron as I could carry and made a trap to lure the creature into."

"Did this work?"

"Yes, my lord," Rowan said motioning towards the bucket on the floor. "I was able to lure it into a trap and get the iron wrapped around it.  Once it was subdued, I tried to kill it.

"What do you mean 'tried' to kill it?" asked the jarl. "Wouldn't the iron kill it?"

"No, my lord. I tried to bury my ax in its head but it did not kill the creature."

"Did you hit it hard enough?" asked a man.

"Yes, I sunk the ax deep into it. You can see where on its head," Rowan said pointing at the bucket.

"How did you kill it?" he asked.

"When I chopped its head off instead, its body went limp and died. Only its head remained alive."

"Where is its body now?" ask the lawspeaker.

"I piled wood over its body and burned it."

"Why?" asked the lawspeaker with a look of concern.

184

"It was the only way I could be sure it would not come back to life," said Rowan.

"What made you think it would not just come back to life after you burned it?" said the old lawspeaker.

"Because was not able to move the body and bury it. I figured burning it would be the best way to keep it from coming back."

"It was a wise move," Jarl Erling said. "To burn the body. That way there would be no way the creature could come back or have its body searching for its head."

The thought horrified Rowan.

After hearing Rowan's story, the men in the hall began debating among themselves and exchanging their own personal feelings on the matter. Some were deciding whether or not they believed Rowan's story.

The head he brought back was undeniable proof that he slayed the creature. The fact that the head was still alive was also proof it was indeed the creature.

It was undeniably something unnatural and it seemed to bother the old lawspeaker immensely.

After a few moments, the jarl finally stood up and got everybody's attention.

"Quiet men," he said, "we've heard the thrall's account and he indeed has brought proof of the creature's death..."

He looked down at the head in the bucket.

"Well, the creature's mostly death," he said, "as the head somehow remains alive. We must now hear what Alvis the Lawspeaker has to say after hearing all of this."

Jarl Erling stood up and turned towards the Alvis the lawspeaker.

"Tell us wise one," he said. "What do you know of such things. Would he have been able to end this creature and why is the head still alive. Tell us what black magic this is that keeps the abomination's head alive?"

The lawspeaker spoke as loud as his frail elderly voice would allow.

"I think it came for vengeance," Alvis said, "I think I may recognize..."

"Never mind that," snapped the jarl. "What is important is whether or not the creature will return again.  Is it dead?"

"I do not know why this creature's head is still alive," the old man said. "That is something of knowledge that perhaps the Völva would be able to tell us."

"I agree," said the jarl. "We will have to send for the völva from the neighboring village and see what knowledge she has of this creature, if any."

The old man nodded his head in agreement.

"She may know why we were plagued by this creature and perhaps know if it has been stopped from returning."

The Jarl raised an eyebrow and nodded his head.

The old man then turned towards Rowan and said, "it was a good thing you didn't just bury it. The creature probably would have risen again, with or without its head."

"I agree," said the jarl. "Even though its head remains alive, it may not be able to return now that its body has been reduced to ash."

He turned and looked at Rowan.

"Did you know there was a reward for killing it?" he asked.

"No, my lord," Rowan said. "I am not aware of any reward for killing the creature. I just knew it I had to do something."

It was true. Rowan wasn't aware of any kind reward or what exactly that meant. This was new information to him and was somewhat puzzling to him as well.

"Someone fetch the blacksmith's widow, Gwenda Helgasdottir. She is the one that owns this thrall and she needs to be here. She must know that her son and husband's deaths have been avenged. Someone bring her here at once!"

"I shall get her, my lord," said a guard in the back of the hall before swiftly exiting out the door.

It wasn't very long until Gwenda arrived with the guard. Although the wait seemed even longer to Rowan as his mind ran through different scenarios as to what his fate was going to be. He was now regretting ever going off into the forest and slaying the creature at this point.

The men in the hall hushed as Gwenda walked past them in the hall towards the jarl.

"Bring her a chair," said the jarl to one of his thralls.

The thrall quickly grabbed a chair and brought it to Gwenda, who noticed the head in the bucket as she sat down. She immediately cowered from it and was openly repulsed.

"My pardons lady for not having that put up before you entered," the Jarl said.

Without needing the jarl's instruction, a guard appeared with a cloth and used it to cover the bucket so she wouldn't be forced to look at it.

"Thank you," she said to the guard.

Secretly, the Jarl was glad for her arrival and for having an excuse to cover up the repulsive thing.

"My dear lady," said the jarl. "That is the head that belonged to the beast that is responsible for slaying your son and husband. They have been avenged."

"Thank you, my lord," she said. "Thank you for reaping vengeance on behalf of my family."

She stood up and faced the men in the hall and addressed them all.

"My greatest gratitude to the hero of our folk who has slain this beast and rid our people of any further harm from it," she said.

She looked around at all the faces in the hall to see who would come forward to state that they were the one who slayed the creature and avenged her family, but nobody did.

"Please hero," she plead, "show yourself. My family owes you the greatest of our gratitude."

Jarl Erling stood up and approached Gwenda and put his hand on her shoulder.

"My fair lady," he said, "your hero is your very own thrall."

He pointed at Rowan, who was still kneeling and looking down at the ground not sure what to do or say.

"My thrall?"

"Lady, did you send your thrall out to slay the creature?"

"No, my lord.  I did not," she said. "We were out trading all day and weren't even aware our thrall was missing until we came home to find him gone."

Rowan's heart sank. Just what he needed, to be accused of trying to escape again. That was an offense punishable by death if his master or mistress so desired.

Jarl Erling stood up and addressed the hall.

"The thrall named Rowan," he said, "without permission from his mistress nor with the intent of collecting the bounty for slaying the draug that was plaguing our village, has took it upon himself to go out alone and kill the wretched thing."

*"Here it comes," thought Rowan, "I'm going to be accused of escaping."*

"He did so with no plan for compensation or reward," said the jarl. "He did this for the better of our people and of this village. He has achieved alone what none of our best men could achieve. This is a selfless and heroic act that must be recognized!"

There were cheers of approval from the men within the hall. The announcement surprised Rowan, who just a moment ago was expecting the worse and was even starting to regret killing the beast.

Jarl Erling stepped in front of Rowan and commanded, "Rise thrall!"

Rowan nervously rose to his feet, still unsure as to what was about to happen.

"Late last night after your mistress left with you, I placed a bounty of 500 silver pieces to whomever slayed the beast that plagued my jarldom," he said to Rowan.

Jarl Erling turned towards the men in the hall.

"Because of this thrall's selfless act of bravery, he is no longer worthy of being that of a mere thrall," he said. "That would be a disgrace to our own people. With the bounty I placed on the beast, I pay his mistress the weregeld value of a useful thrall of 60 silver pieces."

A guard stepped next to the jarl and handed him a fine leather bag full of silver pieces.

The jarl counted out 60 pieces of silver from it

and handed it to Gwenda.

Confused, she took the silver and sat there bewildered with an uncertain look on her face. She was relieved to have the deaths of her son and husband revenged, but she didn't expect to lose her thrall. This was a problem, but she knew she could not speak up against the jarl's decision.

"Having paid for ownership of the thrall as property of my own," the jarl said. "I announce before everyone that I free him and that he is no longer a thrall. The man named Rowan is now a freeman."

Some of the men immediately protested this decision while others cheered for it. There hall began to get louder and louder, until the jarl made another announcement.

"Not only do I make him a new freed man," he said, "I make him a karl among our people."

Many of the men loudly voiced their protest.

"I do this because he has proven himself as a hero and braver than any other man I have seen in my realm."

"He is not a karl," said one man.

"He is just a mere thrall," complained another.

"How is that fair to our folk?" grumbled another.

192

This last statement caused some of the men to argue within the hall. This angered Jarl Erling and he immediately put an end to it.

"I have seen not one man do what this man has done," he said. "He has earned the status and the right and not a single man here can argue against that, lest he disgrace himself and the people of my realm."

Jarl Erling turned towards one of his guards and pointed at Rowan.

"Have his neck ring removed at once,"he said, "he is no longer a thrall!"

He then turned towards the men in the hall and said, "we will celebrate his honor!"

Rowan stood there still in shock of what had just happened. Jarl Erling walked over to him and handed him the sack of silver.

He didn't know what to do or say and just looked up at the jarl with a confused look.  The jarl took hold of his hand and placed the sack in his hand.

"The remaining reward bounty is yours, Rowan."

Rowan looked down of the small bag of silver in his hand. He was stunned. He'd never possessed or even held money before.

Jarl Erling chuckled and slapped him on the

shoulder.

"You're welcome," he said.

"Yes, my lord, " Rowan quickly said. "Thank you very much."

The Jarl turned and returned to his throne. A few men stepped forward and patted Rowan on the back, congratulating him. It was a strange feeling to him. He'd never been treated as an equal or even acknowledged him as a human being.  Now they were treating him as one of their own.

Well some of them.  Many continued to scowl and looked at him with contempt.

One man came in with tools and removed the pin from Rowan's neck ring. He pulled it off and handed it to the jarl.

Jarl Erling walked up to Gwenda, who'd been quietly sitting in her chair flabbergasted, and handed her the neck ring and her husband's ax.

"I believe these belong to you fair lady," he said.

She took them from the jarl and quietly left.

The jarl grabbed a drinking horn from one of the thralls walking by and handed it to Rowan, who was still looking down at the bag of silver and feeling unusually 'naked' due to no longer wearing his neck ring.

He looked up and accepted the Jarl's offer of mead.

"Thank you my lord."

The jarl satisfied, turned towards the rest of the men in the hall and said, "drink up everyone and feast at my table."

He turned back towards Rowan and pointed at the main table in the hall where various meats among other foods were being set up by his thralls.

"Eat and be merry as my guest,"he said. "You are a hero Rowan. Perhaps tomorrow, you will swear your allegiance to me and receive your arm ring."

"Yes my lord."

Rowan looked around the hall and saw the World for the first time through the eyes of a freeman.

Things were different now.  He was going to have to learn how to live as a karl and make a life for himself.

But tonight not tonight.  Tonight, he was drinking from the jarl's horn s an honored guest.

A thrall brought him a chunk of meat and some bread.  It was one of the best cuts, something reserved only for the jarl.  He savored it.

Up high in the rafters in a dark corner, unnoticed

by anyone in hall, quietly sat the wee Tom Taye.  He
was quite pleased with himself as he watched his
plan played itself out perfectly.

But there was still much to do.

# Chapter 13

The fires in the jarl's hall burned through the night long after the last merrymaker spilled the last horn of mead.  The hall was large enough on its own, but the shadows that were cast from the light glowing from the fires made it look even larger.

It was a grand hall that had been built by Jarl Erling's father, Rovald "the Earless."  He'd acquired the nickname *Earless* when a thrown spear nicked his shield and sliced his left ear off.  It happened in the battle that was fought for control of these very lands.

Rovald had mustered a force with his brother Argun and seized the lands from Jarl Ingvald in a surprise dawn attack launched from the forest.  The Jarl's housekarls fought well, but eventually they were overwhelmed by the attackers when they set fire to the hall.

Heavily wounded, Jarl Ingvald was forced to flee into the forest with his son and surviving family members where he died. They gave a him a hasty funeral in the hills and then the defeated jarl's son and his pregnant wife fled south across the seas with some of the survivors still loyal.

Jarl Ingvald's grief stricken wife refused to leave her husband's graveside.

Upon hearing about Jarl Ingvald's death, Rovald named himself as jarl and had the new hall built over the burnt ruins of the old one.  They built the new hall using timber from the woods from where they launched their attack from.

The hall's ornamented setstokkr beams were personally selected and blessed by the völva with the blood of the fallen. There had been a feast that lasted over a month with several ceremonies, including when Argun arraigned the marriage of his son Bjord.

Years later, Jarl Rovald found out where the previous jarl's heirs had escaped and sent a raiding force led by Argun to kill them.  He wanted to prevent them from ever returning in force to claim their lands back.

His brother Argun was killed in the raid. When they returned to tell Jarl Rovald, he became grief stricken and fell ill.  He died shortly after naming his son Erling as heir.

Everyone knew the tale well because it was told

every year during Midwinter along with other sagas.

It had been again told last night by Alvis the lawspeaker before he retired for the night.

Rowan woke with a terrible pain in his head. He feasted on the richest portions of meats and indulged many kinds of sweetbreads.

His sweet tooth had always been a weakness of his, but nevertheless it was the mead that had done him in.

He slept the night on one of the large benches that ran along the side of the jarl's hall. These benches were wider than the benches at the tables in the center of the hall. They were also covered with soft furs and wool blankets. Some of the finest to be found in the area.

It was the most comfortable bedding that Rowan had ever slept on. This was how the jarl's personal guard, the housekarls, lived. Jarl Erling made sure those most loyal to him were well taken care of.

Rowan's previous existence as a thrall was not the most luxurious. Although his master the blacksmith had treated him well, his bedding was only slightly better than that of the livestock. He'd always slept on beds made of straw with old patched blankets since he sold to the blacksmith.

But that life was over.

Rowan was now welcomed in the jarl's hall as one of his honored guests.  He was now a karl, a freeman.

It also seemed that Jarl Erling favored him by calling him a hero. This probably placed him in a position to climb in status. In fact, Rowan was now hoping to become one of the Jarl's Housekarls. He really had no other plans and this was how the Jarl's Housekarl Guard lived.

Rowan had already spent some of the silver that he got last night from the jarl trading for some new clothes and a few other items. Not many of the locals would trade fairly with him, being who he was, but in the end silver was silver.

He wanted to visit the home of his former master and purchase an ax, but with the amount of distance and resistance he was getting from the locals, he felt that it would be a bad idea.  He was instead forced to pay too much for an old chipped ax from an unwilling fisherman.

The old fisherman also made Rowan help him outstretch his fishing net for mending before he'd make the trade.

It took much of the afternoon to do.

# Chapter 14

It was late in the day when the völva had arrived with a small entourage which included the Jarl's wife, Auga and her personal escort of housekarls and servants.

Auga had been away at the neighboring village visiting her sister when she heard word of the völva being summoned by her husband the jarl.  She accompanied the völva and her nine assistants who were pulling the völva in a cart which was decorated with massive elk horns wrapped with flower blossoms.

The young girls pulling the cart wore fur hoods and were stained crimson head to toe.

Despite the small coven of young servants, the völva was also accompanied by two older women who were dressed in rune decorated gowns.

The old seeress herself wore a long white dress

that was as white as her frayed unbraided hair. She had a long fur cloak made from a clowder of cats draped over her shoulders.

The cloak had various gems that were sewn into its hem. Around her neck was a string of lustrous white and bluish-gray stones. A large amber gem called the 'Eye of Loki' hung in the center. The sprig of an ancient mistletoe was said to be within its center.

The two women helped the old woman out of the cart and led her into the Jarl's Hall. Many curious onlookers gawked as she walked past them with the assistance of a long distaff and one of her lady attendants.

She came before the Jarl as he stood up from his throne and formally greeted her.

"Welcome wise Völva of the Hard Fjord. Voice of the gods, seeress of all, your guidance is most welcome in my hall. Please sit in my chair as our most honored guest!"

The old seeress stepped up and sat down on the jarl's throne. Jarl Erling scurried to get a cushion and placed it behind her back in his chair. He turned towards one of thralls and pointed towards his chambers.

"Thrall! Fetch some wine," he said. "Get the good

wine I have hidden in my chambers and get the finest of our meats!"

He turned back towards the old woman now comfortably seated in his chair and knelt down before her on one knee.  He took her hand into his and said, "thank you for answering our call, wise seeress of the gods."

"What troubles you noble jarl?" she said. "Why have you summoned for me?"

"There has been a great darkness cast upon us. An ancient magic that has summoned the enmity of a draug. We seek your vision and your wisdom, dear völva."

The jarl reached into his belt and removed a small pouch and placed it in the völva's hand.  She took it and tucked it away on her person.

As if on queue, some of the younger women who had stayed outside came into the hall carrying drums.  The old woman stood up from the jarl's chair and called out to the gods while raising her distaff in the air.

A couple superstitious men darted out the door, calling it an early night.

She started swaying in a sort of trance-like state. Two younger women moved to each side of her and began tapping on their drums.

They began swaying in rhythm with her.

The old woman began chanting in some unknown tongue as she traced symbols in the air with her strange looking distaff that was wrapped in strains of gold and silver.  The gems on the knob seemed to glitter as she did so.

The women with her began to softly sing as they continued tapping on their drums and swaying side to side.

It was quite a spectacle and most of the hall was captivated by it.  Even Rowan just stood there in awe watching them.

A couple more men scurried out the hall's door without looking back.

The völva reached into a small red pouch made from otter pelt that she had fastened to her belt by a gold ring. She took out a handful of flat river stones and tossed them on the ground in front of her.

Immediately, she flung herself down on her hands and knees and began swaying over the stones she just cast on the floor.  The stones had golden runes written on them.  She picked one of them up and held it in the air and gurgled something indistinguishable.  She reached down and grabbed another and held it up towards the Jarl.

"Your blood it seeks!" she said.

Her accomplices immediately stopped chanting and set their drums down. They walked over to the old woman and helped her back up to her feet.

She began shouting in a raspy voice as she held up the rune stones, one in each hand, towards everyone in the hall.

"The one who cannot rest must be pinned to its resting place with iron until it no longer rages." she said.

She turned around and looked directly at Jarl Erling and said, "it will rage until its line is returned to its place."

She started swaying again with her head tilted and eyes rolled into the back of her head.

Another man ran towards the door and fell to the ground, tripping over his own feet. Nobody laughed as he quickly got up and headed out of the hall.

Her eyes returned to normal as she tilted her head back and looked directly at Rowan.

"It was the scent of his blood that it found," she said. "But he has a different destiny he must seek."

Everyone in the hall turned and looked at Rowan.

"He was the one who slew the creature and sent it back to Hel's kingdom," said Alvis. "It has been slain."

"Is that the voice of Alvis the Wise that I hear?" she said.

"It is." said the old lawspeaker.

"Then you should know that you cannot simply kill what is already dead."

"The creature was slain and its head has been removed..." he said.

"The beast will come back," she said. "It will keep coming back until it has been freed."

"Tell us wise seeress," said the jarl, "what do we do?"

"It must be staked to its resting place by iron," she said. "If it is staked to its resting place with iron, it cannot rise."

"But it is clearly dead," said the jarl, "we have its head."

"It is not dead," she said. "It has only been slowed down and it will eventually come back. It is controlled by a dark hatred and it is obsessed with its task. It seeks to kill the one that..."

The old völva abruptly stopped talking and

started choking.

She quickly regained her composure and tried to speak, but started choking again.

When she didn't stop coughing, her assistants came to her aid and offering her a drink of warmed mead.

The old woman took the drink and after a minute waved off her attendants and cleared her throat.

"The creature is obsessed with killing..."

She started choking again before she could finish her sentence.

The poor old woman was choking so hard that her face began to redden. She dropped down to her knees and held her throat as she started coughing even harder. Her assistants rushed to her side just as she spewed blood on the ground in front of her.

"Quick, get her some water!" Jarl Erling ordered one of his thralls standing nearby.

She looked up and took in one final breath before her face contorted into a frozen gasp of agony as she fell forward onto the ground, dead.

One of her assistants screamed as the other one beside her fainted and fell on top of her.

Jarl Erling stepped up to the women's bodies and

rolled the younger fainted woman off the old
woman's body with his foot.  He knelt down and
examined the old woman on the floor, rolling her to
her side to get a better look at her.

"She's dead," he said.

"What kind of sorcery is this?!" said Alvis.

Jarl Erling stood up and turned to look at
everyone in the hall. Everyone was wide-eyed and
frightened at what they'd just seen. They started
looking around at each other trying to figure out
who or what may have cast the spell killing the old
völva.

Accusations spread across the hall as they began
pointing fingers at each other.

"He's the one she said awakened it!" said one
man pointing at Rowan.

"She said it found his scent," said another, "but
he is not the one that it seeks."

"I find it very suspicious that he was even able to
survive," said Thorn. "Look at him. He is no
warrior."

"Silence!" shouted Jarl Erling. "I will not have
any of that in my hall! He was standing right here in
front of everyone, we know he did not do it. There
was no magic. The völva was old.

"Not that old," said Thorn, "that wasn't natural."

"She was old when I was a boy," said Alvis. "But I agree, that was not natural."

The woman who fainted came to and began weeping while the other tried to comfort her.

"My ladies of the seeress," said Jarl Erling. "I am profoundly sorry for your loss."

He called over a couple of his guards.

"Wrap her body so that she may be carried out," he instructed them.

"Thank you noble jarl," she said as the other women walked up and gathered the old woman's body. "But that will not be necessary."

The women picked up the völva's body and carried it out the door. Auga, the jarl's wife, followed them outside.

"My lord," said Hakon, "what shall we to do?"

"I will have a couple of my men escort them until they don't need them any longer."

"Should we help with the burial?"

"They have their own ways which are closed to men," he said, "they will perform the burial far from us."

"Don't we need to send a man to notify someone about her death?"

"They already know," said Alvis.

Jarl Erling removed the cushion he'd brought the völva, tossed it to a thrall and sat in his chair for a few minutes quietly thinking.

Finally he stood up and addressed everyone in the hall.

"Someone must go to the creature's burial mound and hammer a rod of iron into it," he said. "The creature must be prevented from returning until we can find a way to lift the curse."

"I agree," said Alvis. "The draug will eventually return.  It must be pinned to its grave or this village may never have any peace from it."

Jarl Erling stood up.

"Who among you will see to this task?" asked the Jarl

He looked around at the men in the hall, but nobody stepped forward.

"I will see to this task, my lord," said Rowan. "But I will need a rod of iron and a hammer to pound it into the mound."

"Does anyone have an iron rod and hammer that

can be used?" said the jarl.

"He can use me hammer!" hollered a man from the back of the hall.

"Very good," said the jarl. "Does anybody have an iron rod?"

"I have some iron spikes that can be used," said a man.

"Will iron spikes work?" he asked Rowan.

"No," Hakon said. "The iron rod should be at least half the length of a man, maybe longer."

Rowan nodded in agreement.

"Is the mound that large?" said the jarl.

"Yes, my lord," said Hakon.

"It should at least be half the length of a man to make sure it penetrates the grave." said Alvis.

"Who has an iron rod long enough?" ask the jarl.

"What about using a spear?"

"No, it must be solid iron. A spear is only iron on the end and then wood." said Alvis.

"I have a rod that will work." said the voice of an old woman in the back of the hall.

It was grandmother Helga, Gwenda's mother.

She'd been sitting in the back the whole time quietly watching.

The old woman stood up from her fur cushion on the bench and held up an iron distaff.

Jarl Erling walked over to her and took the iron distaff from her hand and looked at it.

"Yes," he said. "This would work, but it looks quite old.  Are you sure you want to part with it, dear grandmother?"

"Yes, it is quite old my lord.  It was given to me by my grandmother."

"Oh, it is too old dear grandmother, we couldn't possibly..."

"Yes, you must," she said. "This creature must be pinned to its grave. I have other distaffs."

"You are a very generous grandmother. The whole of our kindred thank you for helping us put an end to this accursed abomination," he said.

He turned to walk away, but noticed something on the distaff and turned back around.

"What is this writing on it?" said Jarl Erling. "I recognize the old runes. My grandfather taught them to me, but I cannot make out the words."

"They were carved on the distaff before my time

in a language almost forgotten," she said.

The Jarl nodded and dropped the matter.

"It is settled.," he announced as he walked back to his chair. "Rowan will take this rod and drive it into the beast's mound."

"Here is the hammer," said a man as he handed the jarl a blacksmithing hammer.

"Thank you," said the jarl. " I will make sure it returns to you."

Jarl handed the hammer and iron distaff to Rowan.

"I don't envy your task," he said as he patted Rowan on the shoulder before walking back to his chair.

"My lord," said Helga as the jarl sat down. "What of my grandson and son in law's bodies?  And those of the other men?"

Jarl Erling gave her a puzzled look.

"My lord," she said, "shouldn't their bodies be brought back so they may have proper funerals and be amongst their kin and kindred before them?"

"Yes,"he said, "we will need to retrieve the bodies."

He stood up and addressed the Hall.

"I need some men to go up to the draug's mound with Rowan and help carry the bodies of our fellow kin back so they may enter the afterlife properly."

The Jarl's Hall was quiet.

"Nobody huh?"

"We mean no offense, my lord, " said a man. "The last men to go up there died."

Jarl Erling ignored him.

"I need twelve men of this village to go up that mountain side and collect the bodies of their kinsmen," he said.

Nobody.

"I will not ask again," he said loudly. "There will be twelve men outside of this hall in the morning to accompany Rowan and bring our kinsmen home."

The Jarl angrily turned and stormed off to his chambers.

The hall was quiet as many men just stood there looking down in shame.

Auga came inside and looked around in the Hall.

"You men should be ashamed of yourselves. You serve the jarl and this village. A mere thrall shows more bravery than the whole lot of you. Perhaps we should send women instead to do this task."

She looked around one last time and she too, turned and went into the jarl's chambers.

"I will go," said Hakon. "I have seen the beast with my own eyes and I also have seen its slain head with my own eyes.  There is nothing to fear in the forest near its mound. The creature has been slain and we must gather the bodies of our kinsmen and bring them home. Who joins me?"

Two more men stepped forward, as did some of the jarl's housekarls, and took their place with him.

A heavyset man stepped forward and stood beside them.

"You're no warrior," mocked someone. "Sit back down where the food is."

Several men in the hall began laughing.

"I know I am no warrior," he said, "but we are not going to battle. We are going to bring our fallen kinsmen home."

The laughter instantly ceased.

"He's right," said a man. "There will be enough men outside of the hall in the morning. The Jarl needn't worry."

Rowan looked down at the iron distaff and hammer.  It was a good hammer with a slightly worn head and a solid handle. The distaff seemed strange to him. He'd seen grandmother Helga with it on several occasions. It was her favorite distaff.  In fact, she was usually carrying this distaff around with her and using it as a walking stick.

He'd never really held it before and was surprised by how heavy it felt, especially being carried around all the time by an old woman.

He didn't recall ever seeing the runes carved on it before, but this was the first time he'd ever held it and looked at it very close. Either way, it didn't matter.  What did matter was that he had to go up to the mound again.

The gravity of what he'd volunteered to do had suddenly just hit him and his shoulders sunk.

He looked up in the direction of Helga and noticed that she was watching him examine the iron distaff.

She smiled and looked at him with a sparkle of mischief in her eyes.

# Chapter 15

Jarl Erling went into his chambers and poured himself a horn of wine from an urn that was set on a table near the wall.

Auga followed him into the bed chamber. She watched him fill the horn with wine and guzzle it down.

Something was definitely bothering him.

She motioned for the chambermaid to leave.

"What was that all about?" he said.

The jarl stared at his drinking horn without turning around.

"What do you mean," she asked.

"Challenging my men like that," he said as he turned around. "Saying that the women should be sent instead and then comparing them to a thrall."

"I was only trying to inspire them to do what they knew they needed to do," she said.

He slammed the drinking horn down on the table and angrily took a step towards her.

"Do you not realize what has been going on in my lands? Do you not realize that as jarl, it is my responsibility to protect these people. I do not need you complicating things."

Auga was about to say something, then stopped short and looked down into her empty hands.

"I am sorry, my love," she said. "I had no idea I was making matters worse."

"Something has cursed my lands and the people are fearful.  They are pointing fingers and have become suspicious of everything - including me!" he shouted.

A baby could be heard crying in the adjoining room.  It was the Jarl's son, Garth.

Auga went into the other room and re-emerged holding a baby, trying to sooth him.

It wasn't her son, Auga had only been married to Jarl Erling for a couple months. His previous wife had passed away while giving birth to his son, Garth.  Auga adopted him as her own when she was married to the jarl by her uncle a month later.

Jarl Erling had two other sons who drowned when they were out fishing.  A storm had suddenly came upon them and capsized their boat. The jarl's wife was pregnant with his son Garth at the time.

The loss of his sons and then losing his wife shortly after had changed him profoundly.

Auga soothed the baby by dipping her pinky finger in some wine and then stuck it in the baby's mouth to suckle.

"My love," she said, "there is no reason to get upset. It is not you they are suspicious of."

"Oh they aren't, are they? Then tell me, who are they suspicious of?" he said in a lower tone as to not make the baby cry again.

She didn't answer and continued soothing the baby.

He walked across the room and sat down on a bear skin covered bench.

"You have not even been here," he said. "Tell me this great insight you have of what's been going on in my lands while you have been absent."

"My love," she said, "there is no reason to be hostile. You know the words of women travel much faster than the words of men."

"I suppose you are right," he said.

He rubbed his eyes and leaned forward to stare at the floor.

"A wise man knows to listen to his wife."

"And that is exactly why I know what's going on in your lands," she said as she sat next to him. "I was informed of everything before I even made it all the way back."

He looked at her and she simply smiled back.

"I don't like how everyone is sneaking behind my back," he said. "It's as if everyone is plotting and seeking my demise."

"That is not so, my love. I was only informed because of the dangers that had come to your lands. They told me - "

"They? Who are *they*?"

"Some of the women. It is not important. What *is* important is that they informed me not only of what had been taking place" she said, "but more importantly what people are saying about it."

"Ah-ha, here it comes," he said sarcastically. "And what are they saying, pray tell?"

"They say it's all because of that thrall you freed."

"That thrall I freed?" he said.

He stood up from the bench and took a few steps

226

before turning around and facing her.

"That thrall that I freed is the very same thrall that killed the beast and rid us of its menace. Something no other man was able to do. Is that the thrall you're referring to?"

She looked away without answering.

Jarl Erling turned away from her and began pacing across the room for a few moments until finally he stopped in front of her.

"That former thrall, his name is Rowan by the way, is also the very same man who is going to make sure that thing doesn't come back."

"Yes, I know, but..."

"But nothing," he said. "Nobody in my lands needs to question my rule or the decisions I make. Otherwise they can meet the sharp end of my sword!"

He turned away from her and started pacing again.

"It is not that," she said. "They think the reason the beast came in the first place is because of the thrall, not because of you my love."

He stopped pacing and studied her face.

"They not only believe that it came for him

specifically," she said, "but that he may have used some kind of sorcery to bring it call the beast from its grave."

"That's nonsense."

"Is it?" she said. "As you pointed out, he was the only one able to kill it and then when the völva was about to reveal its connection to him, she dies before she can speak.  You don't find that suspicious?"

"She was old," he said.

"I agree. She was probably as old as time itself. But you must agree that it wasn't a normal death. That was some kind of sorcery and it had to be extremely powerful because the völva was the most powerful seeress in all the North lands."

"Nonsense."

"My love," she said. "Whether it is nonsense or not, that is what the people believe."

"They do not know what they are talking about."

"Even still, they wholeheartedly believe it and they also..."

She stopped talking and looked away.

"They what?" he demanded.

"They say you favor this thrall."

228

"Of course I favor Rowan," he said. "He has
killed the draug. He done what all the other karls
and housekarls of this village have failed to do. That
is why I emancipated him from thralldom and made
him a karl.  Nobody can question that."

"Yes, I understand. But they not only worry that
he may have used sorcery, but your people feel that
he has been risen to a place higher than them and he
was but a mere thrall."

"That is their problem.  Besides, he can take care
of himself.  If they have a problem with him then
they can take it to him."

"They will not."

"What do you mean?"

"I am told your captain of the housekarls, Hakon,
protects the thrall."

She got up and slowly walked across the room
holding the baby and stepped into the doorway to
call the chambermaid back in.

She came in and Auga handed her the baby.  The
girl dutifully took the child and quietly returned to
the adjoining chamber with him.

"Send him away for a few days," Auga said as
soon as the chambermaid was out of the room.

"Send him away," he asked. "Rowan?"

"No my love," she said, "your captain of the housekarls. Have him escort the völva's body back to her coven and then let me take care of this problem thrall of yours."

"I need him to escort Rowan and some of the men to stake that iron rod into the draug's resting mound and..."

"Yes, my love. I meant when they return."

"They will have already left by then," he said.

"They mentioned something to me about having to prepare the path or something like that," she said. "They said they cannot leave until tomorrow night."

"Tomorrow night?"

"Yes," she said. "They've place her body in that cart and have been standing around her tapping on their drums."

What are they doing?" he said.

"They are preparing her body for her journey they said and they won't take any food or drink until after she completes her journey."

"Her journey?" he said. "What does that even mean?"

"I don't know," she said. "All I know is they intend to leave tomorrow evening when the sun sets."

"When the sun sets," he asked. "Why then?"

"They said, 'for her path to be lit, the world must first be darkened'."

Jarl Erling just gave her a puzzled look.

She just smiled and shrugged her shoulders.

"How do you plan to deal with Rowan, he's not a thrall any longer. You simply cannot murder him now."

"Yes yes, I know," she said. "Let me worry about that. But your people, my love, they believe that he may be the very reason that draug came in the first place. They will not leave it be while he's still here."

"I'm not so sure."

"What do you mean you're not so sure?" she said. "It came after him didn't it, but yet it did not kill him. It killed others, but not him.  And then when some of your best warriors go against it, this untrained thrall with no battle experience is the only one able to kill it? That seems awfully suspicious to me."

"I know, I know," he said. "Do you think I don't hear what the people in my own lands are saying, woman?  Especially within the walls of my own hall?"

*'Apparently not,'* she thought.

"It must be done." she said. "I will handle it and your hands will be clean.  Then your lands can return to the peacefulness that existed before all this started. Your rule, my love, will be secure."

He stood there a few moments studying her face before finally nodding and turning to leave.

"My love," she said just as he was at the doorway. "Do not worry, leave it to me."

He left the chamber and returned to the main hall.

# Chapter 16

It was early the next morning when Rowan woke up to Hakon nudging him with his foot.

"Come on," he said. "It's time to go."

Rowan sat up and stretched as Hakon walked off to wake the other men. He reached over and grabbed a basin that had been filled with water by one of the jarl's thralls. He scooped up some water and washed the sleep out of his eyes.

The other men in the hall that Hakon had risen were doing similar as they collected themselves.

One man approached Rowan from behind as he was fastening his belt and said, "why does this thrall have to go with us?"

Hakon stepped behind him and said, "he's the one that's going to drive the iron rod into the draug's mound. Unless, of course, you want to do it in his place?"

The man didn't answer and walked away.

"By order of the jarl, Rowan is no longer a thrall and is no longer to be regarded as one. He is a karl." said Hakon to nobody particular as he headed out the door.

The other men began to slowly follow behind.

Rowan gathered the iron distaff, the hammer, and the chipped ax that smelled of fish that he'd got from the old fisherman.

Thirteen men along with Hakon and Rowan, made a total of fifteen men that gathered outside of the jarl's hall for this task.

Hakon noticed that many of the men were putting on armor and getting their weapons ready.

"There's no need to worry about arming up," he said. "We're going to fetch the fallen, not go to battle."

Hakon turned and began waking towards the blacksmith's longhouse to get to the path in the forest leading to the mound.

"I noticed you brought your sword," said Jorgen, one of the jarl's housekarls who'd volunteered to come.

Hakon paid no mind to the man's remark and kept walking.

Rowan and the other men followed behind him. Most of the men made sure to carry at least some form of weapon and shield, just in case.

They entered the woods and walked quietly in a single file with Hakon leading and Rowan behind him. The trail to the mound no longer needed to be tracked and was starting to become a path.

Hakon stopped and picked up a branch. The end of it was burned.

"Someone's been through here," he said.

Rowan looked at it, puzzled at first, but then remembered.

"That was mine," he said. "When I came down, I made a torch and had tossed it aside when it died out."

Hakon tossed it to the side and continued following the path towards the mound.

Rowan noticed something moving out of the corner of his eye. Something darted behind the trees and it looked like it was that strange blond haired lady that he'd seen in the woods before.

Without drawing the attention of anyone else, he tried to catch a better glimpse of her.

"Hey," Jorgen said, "did you see that?"

He stopped walking and pointed at a clump of trees.

"Look," he said, "over there."

Everybody stopped walking and looked in the direction he was pointing. It was where Rowan thought he'd caught a glimpse of the woman.

"What?" said Hakon.

"Over there."

Jorgen pointed towards the trees again.

"I saw something."

Hakon looked where he was pointing.

"What is it?" said Hakon. "What did you see?"

"I saw a woman over there," he said.

Everyone started laughing and began walking up the trail again.

He turned and looked at everyone.

"I swear, I saw her. There was a woman over there."

"He saw a woman!" someone mocked. "Way out here in the woods!'

"No seriously," he said. "I swear I saw a woman hiding behind those trees over there."

238

Jorgen kept glancing back in the direction trying to see her again.

"I think somebody's had too many lonely nights if they're seeing women coming out of the trees deep in the forest," said Hakon.

The men continued to have a laugh at Jorgen's expense, but he knew he'd seen a naked woman dart behind the trees.

Rowan wasn't laughing. He'd seen her in the corner of his eye too, but he wasn't going to say anything. He had enough problems as it was.

They walked in relative silence after that until they arrived at the clearing just ahead of the draug's mound.

Rowan walked up the where he burned the draug's body, but the remains of the draug's burnt body were missing.

"This is where the beast's body was and where I burned it," he said as he pointed to the pile of ashes and charred wood. "The chain mail and ax heads are here, but any hint of its body are gone."

They walked around and saw that all the bodies of the fallen men were gone as well.

"Where are the bodies," asked Hakon.

"Are you sure this is the right place?" said Jorgen.

"Yes," said Hakon, "this is the right place. Look, their weapons, shields, and even their clothes and boots are still laying where they fell."

He bent down and picked up a missing man's spangenhelm off the ground.

"Were they here when you came here last time?"

"Yes," Rowan said.

Hakon walked over to where Rowan was standing to get a closer look at where the creature was burned.

"Shield wall!"

It took a second for the men's brains to register what Hakon had just said and react.

"Form a shield wall on me now!" he said as he lifted his shield up defensively and pulled out his sword.

They scrambled to him and lined their shields up next to his, forming a wall of shields.

The men without shields, including Rowan, got behind them with their weapons at the ready.

They stood at the ready facing up the hill in the direction towards the draug's mound and nervously looking around for any movement.

After a few minutes, one of the men finally

whispered, "what should we do?"

Hakon wasn't sure what to do and look back in the direction of Rowan.

"I think if we try to fight it," he said, "we will get the same results as last time. The monster is just too strong, we cannot beat it."

"I agree," said Hakon.

"If the beast shows itself, I suggest we just run."

"I don't run from anything." said Jorgen in a gruff voice.

"The beast will tear us to pieces," said Hakon.

"I have ran from it twice now and twice I have escaped it," said Rowan. "It is fast but it doesn't seem to give chase very long."

"I understand why you ran," said Jorgen. "If I were a woman, I would have ran too."

"We cannot beat it," said Hakon. "I have ran from it and escaped too.  By my honor, we tried to beat it down with everything we had and we were swatted around like flies.  If it shows, then we run and come up with a plan to trap it like Rowan had done before."

Most of the men nodded their heads in agreement.

"You can run if you wish," said Jorgen. "I'll make my stand here and go to Valhalla."

"Alright." said Hakon as he lowered his shield. "It doesn't look like anything is coming out."

"What made you jump," someone asked.

""I didn't jump," said Hakon. "Did you see that spot where he said he burned the body."

"Yeah, so?"

"The print on the ground," said Hakon. "It looks like whatever was there, got up and walked away."

Everybody nervously looked around.

Rowan knelt down and untied Helga's iron distaff that he'd slung across his back and pulled out the hammer tucked in belt.

"Let us get this deed done," he said as he walked around the men and up towards the bushes leading to the draug's mound.

He looked through the torn bushes and stared at the burial mound. His sudden burst of courage left him and he hesitated going through.

The results have always been unpleasant when it came to approaching that burial mound.  But he must finish this task and hammer the iron rod into the center of the mound.  The creature will probably never rise again, he knows he burned it. But there was absolutely no sense in taking any chances.

This had to be done.

Rowan walked through the path and up towards the mound. He watched for even the slightest movement in the corners of his eyes. His ears were keenly perked for even the slightest sound.

Slowly he walked up to the mound, carefully looking around for any hint of the creature.

A sudden flutter burst behind him in the brush.

Dropping the hammer and iron rod, Rowan turned and ran.

He only ran a few steps when he saw what made the sound.

It was just a bird.

A pheasant had burst out from the brush and fluttered off somewhere behind the bushes when he walked by and spooked it.

Embarrassed, Rowan stopped running and dropped his arms. A couple of the other men nervously laughed.

They almost turned and ran with him.

Rowan walked back and picked up the iron distaff and hammer off the ground. He took one last quick look around and then walked up to the edge of the mound.

He stood there a moment and looked down at the river stones on the mound and remembered Bjord saying something about them being carried up there. The air was still and silent around him. The sounds of the birds and leaves rustling from the wind could not be heard.

There was an eerie stillness around the draug's burial mound.

Rowan took in a deep breath and slowly exhaled as he stepped up on top of the mound. He tuned out everything around him as he walked straight up to the center and took a knee.

He stuck the iron distaff Helga gave them into the draug's mound and raised the hammer to strike it in place.

His muscles locked as he swung the hammer down on the top of the rod.

[*ping*]

A dull ring sounded the hammer's impact as it sunk the other end of the iron distaff into the mound's packed dirt.

[*ping*]

He swung again and sunk it deeper into the

mound.  It felt like he hit a rock or something hard, so he shifted himself in front of it to get a better swing at it.

He swung the hammer down with both hands and hit the rod as hard as he could.

[*PING*]

A loud ring came out from within the mound itself and echoed across the hillside. It was immediately followed by an explosive roar from all the frightened birds that suddenly took off in flight.

The men looking on raised up their shields and tightened up their formation. They looked around in every direction for something to come out at them.

The sound of birds died down and nothing came out.

Rowan dropped the hammer and slowly stood up looking in every direction.

It was became quiet again.

"It is done," he said.

He picked up the hammer and walked towards them.

"It is over," said Hakon while lowering his shield.

The other men also lowered their shields and started looking around a little more relaxed.

Hakon looked back at the piles of clothes and weapons of the missing bodies of the fallen men.

"We need to gather up these weapons and whatever we can and bring them back," he said.

"Yes," said Rowan, "my mistress wants the unfinished coats of mail and ax heads returned."

"Mistress?" said Jorgen. "You see, even in his own mind, he's still a thrall."

"That's enough of that," said Hakon.

"I know," he mocked, "by order of the Jarl."

The men scattered to pick up the weapons, shields, and gear laying around in piles on the ground from the fallen men.

Rowan tucked the hammer in his belt and bent down to gather up the unfinished chain mail shirts that he used to trap the draug. They were covered in ash and bits of char from the fire. The ax heads were scattered in the ash too.

The rope that strung them together had long smoldered to nothing, so he took the hammer and ax from his belt and set them down. He then took off his belt and strung the ax heads through it and slung it over his shoulder.  He picked up the chain mail shirts he rolled into bundles and lifted them on his shoulder as well.

After he picked up the hammer and ax, he stood back up while a man holding a couple shields came up behind him.

"I'll take my hammer back now," he said as he rudely grabbed the hammer out of Rowan's hand.

The man looked at him and sneered but Rowan didn't allow him to bait him and simply said, "thanks for letting me use it to pin the draug's mound."

The man grunted and walked off.

The hostility towards Rowan seemed to be growing among many of the men from the village and for just a brief moment; he regretted any of this ever happening and being freed.

*This would be the last time Rowan regretted his own freedom.*

The men gathered up what they could and began walking back to the village to report what they'd found. There was very little said between them the whole way back.

# Chapter 17

They made their way back before sundown and went inside the hall to report what they'd found.

Many looked at them without saying a word. The fac

"My lord, it is done," said Hakon. "The iron rod has been hammered into the creature's mound."

"Wonderful news!" said the jarl. "We can now rejoice in knowing that the creature can never return."

Hakon stepped up to the jarl and whispered in his ear. Rowan could faintly hear him telling the jarl about the missing bodies and the jarl asking him if he was certain. He wasn't able to hear any more because of the men in hall becoming louder as they congratulated them for going up there and returning safely.

"What about the bodies," asked Thorn. "Where's

my brother's body?"

"They were not able to retrieve the bodies and I am most sorry for that," said the jarl. "They were able to bring back their possessions. My guards will make sure they are returned to their families."

"What happened to the bodies?"

"We don't know," answered Hakon.

"We will toast in their honor!" said the jarl. "Their sacrifice to our people in subduing this menace will never be forgotten."

"We saw something in the woods," said Jorgen.

Hakon turned and shot him a look. He shook his head in disbelief and took a step back.

"My lord," said Jorgen. "I saw something in the woods."

"He saw nothing," said Hakon as he stepped down and sat on a bench.

"I did see something," he said. "It was in the corner of my eye for just second, but I know I saw something."

"What did you see?"

"It was a woman," he said. "I saw a naked woman in the woods."

The men in the hall erupted in laughter.

"I swear," he said, "I saw a naked woman in the forest."

This just made the men laugh harder and start mocking him.

"What he may have seen was the Lady in the Forest," said Alvis from the back of the hall.

"The Lady in the Forest?"

"I've heard rumors of the Lady in the Forest being seen, but never believed them."

"Who is the Lady in the Forest?"

"A forest spirit?"

"Perhaps it was a huldra, or some other forest gaurdian."

"If there are huldra in our woods," Alvis said, "then something has enchanted the forest to attract them and there's no telling what else is there."

"Whatever made the draug to come," Oleg said.

"It started with the thrall," Thorn said pointing at Rowan. "It was peaceful here until that thing came and killed my brother."

"It explains all of this," said Oleg. "The thrall was practicing sorcery to kill his master and brought all this upon us."

"There's no need to get started with all of that superstitious nonsense," said Jarl Erling.

"But what about the völva's death?" said Alvis.

"Oh, not you too," said the jarl. "It's nonsense and you know it!"

"There is no denial," Oleg said, "that something has enchanted our forests. The völva tried to warn us and we've all seen what happened to her with our own eyes."

"That's why he must die!" said Thorn.

The accusing shouts continued until Oleg tried to throw a drinking horn at Rowan and hit the man standing beside him in the side of the head and causing the mead within to spray all over the top of his head and spatter the man behind him.

"Enough," shouted the jarl.

The man behind him grabbed Rowan by the shoulder and spun him around.

"What's wrong with you!" he shouted.

"I didn't throw it," Rowan said, "it was thrown at me!"

"I said enough!" said the jarl.

252

"Shall we will settle this now?" challenged the man.

"Both of you sit down!" shouted the Jarl. "There will be no more of this tonight!"

The hall grew silent as a couple of the jarl's housekarls armed with spears stepped forward.

Two of the völva's attendants came into the hall.

"We are ready to bring the völva to her final resting place," she said. "We thank you for your hospitality and the gods smile upon you and your people."

"Please allow me to send an escort to ensure the safety of you and your company," the jarl said.

"There is no need most gracious jarl, we walk with the gods and the gods walk with us."

"Then at least allow me to send a small compliment to show you to the neighboring lands."

"If it pleases you," she said with a bow.

"Hakon," said the jarl. "I have a task for you, my captain of the Housekarl Guard."

"Yes, my lord." Hakon said as he stepped to the jarl.

"Hakon!" said Jarl Erling as he pat him on the shoulder and turned to the völva's attendant. "This is

Hakon, the captain of my Housekarl Guard. He will escort you to the edge of my lands and ensure your safety."

She nodded and gave Hakon a gracious nod before turning and walking away to rejoin her accompaniment outside as they finished preparing the völva's body for transport.

"Hakon," said the jarl. "I know you are tired from just returning, but I need you to take on this task. I need you to take two men with you and escort the völva's funeral procession to the edge of my lands."

Hakon nodded.

"If they need you to escort them all the way, then do so. I have already had my thrall pack rations for a few days just in case this is so."

The jarl walked him over to a bench by the door and showed him the sack of rations and mead flasks.

"It should only take you a few days," the jarl said, "but I must make sure that her body and her attendants leave safely. It already looks bad that she died in my lands."

Hakon nodded, "yes, my lord. I understand."

He turned towards two of the guards and instructed them come with him. They went outside to wait as he gathered his things on the bench before heading out the door to join the völva's company of attendants.

Hakon stepped outside of the jarl's hall and saw that it was already getting dark outside.

The völva's entourage were all carrying torches. There were many of them. Many more than had originally came with her.

There were hundreds of them.

All of them, women, were dressed in white gowns with splatters of red on them and had various floral decorations weaved into their hair.  They all carried a long torch. Hakon could see the line of them leading into the forest as as he could see.

He wondered if there were enough of them to light the entire way.

As soon as he stepped outside, one of the women dressed in white splattered him with something red from a branch she dipped in a bronze bowl that another attendant carried beside her.

Hakon looked up at her and noticed he couldn't see her face. She was wearing a white loose knit veil that just covered her face.

She sprinkled the other two men with Hakon as well. Speechless and feeling uncomfortable, they just looked at each other without saying a word.

Hakon wondered why the Jarl would have sent him to escort these sorceresses. They obviously had nothing to fear in this world.

But he will fulfill his duty.

# Chapter 18

Tensions in the jarl's hall grew off and on throughout the evening. Everyone was very uneasy about all the recent events going on without having any real answers. They only had suspicion fueled by poisonous gossip, which made matters even worse.

Rowan sat off to the side by himself and was pretty much avoided by everyone in the hall. He even had problems with the jarl's thralls not bringing him food or drink. Even they feared him as something supernatural.

Thorn had spent the evening drinking at a table on the other side of the hall. He sat there most of the evening staring at Rowan and bitterly conspiring with Oleg.

"The Jarl should have given me possession of that thrall." sulked Oleg. "He was master-less."

"Oh, I hear ya old friend. My brother's property

should have been passed to me," Thorn said. "That property is a blacksmith's property and now it has no blacksmith."

"I agree," Oleg said.

"No seriously," Thorn stressed, "our father built that blacksmithery and trained both me and my brother in it."

"This village needs its blacksmith back!" Oleg said.

"I should have been given possession of my brother's property. It should have gone to the deceased's only remaining living male kin, which is me!"

The bitterness in Thorn festered deep inside him.

"Something should be done about it," Oleg said.

"Can I fill your horns?" Auga said as she stood behind them holding a mead urn.

Neither of the men said a word. They knew she'd overheard them talking.

Without looking away, Oleg raised his horn up for her to fill.

"You men are correct," she said as she poured mead into his horn. "He must be made an example of so the other thralls don't start getting any ideas."

She turned and began filling Thorn's horn with mead.

"You know my husband will be needing new housekarls for his personal guard. It is a prestigious position at his table that offers certain privileges and rewards," she said just before walking away to offer mead to other men in the hall.

Thorn and Oleg looked at each other for a moment.

"I will find a way to kill the thrall," Thorn said. "An accident or something."

"No, I will do it," Oleg said. "You shouldn't get involved. I think may Gwenda favor the thrall and you don't want to ruin your chances with her. Let me take care of him."

"My chances with her? What do-"

"The whole village knows... You've had your eye on her since you were a wee lad and everyone could see the jealousy in your eyes when she married your brother."

Thorn looked away and took a deep swig of mead from his horn.

"Don't sweat it," he said. "Nobody objects."

Oleg took a finishing gulp from his drinking horn and slammed it on the table and stood up.

"Now watch me pick a fight."

Having been continually ignored by the jarl's thralls, Rowan finally got up and walked over to the fire pit to get some food. He tore off a piece of meat that was hung on an iron spit over the fire and grabbed a drinking horn. He turned towards one of the Jarl's thralls carrying an urn of mead and blocked his path.

Without saying a word, Rowan looked him in the eye and raised the drinking horn up for him to fill it.

The thrall looked down and filled Rowan's horn and then stepped around him to tend to others in the hall.

Rowan took his filled horn and chunk of meat and returned to his seat.

Oleg took notice of Rowan having to serve himself and made his way over to him. He reached down and picked up the chunk of meat that Rowan had just set down and took a bite out of it.

Rowan looked up him and was about to say something, but chose not to and looked away. He knew he was being baited into a fight.

Oleg looked down at him and said, "get me some mead."

"Get your own mead." Rowan said.

262

"Thrall..."

"I am no thrall!" Rowan said as he stood up and faced Oleg.

"I don't think you know where you're going with this thrall," Oleg said as he stared back with anger.

"I am no thrall!"

"That is enough of that!" called out the jarl. "You will not disrespect my Hall!"

Rowan turned and looked at the jarl then looked down.

"Get my mead thrall!" Oleg said again.

Rowan looked back at him in the eyes and calmly said, "get your own mead."

Oleg's hand began creeping up to his belt towards the ax tucked in it.

"How dare the either of you disrespect the hospitality of my hall."

Jarl Erling angrily stood up and then staggered, nearly tripping over his own feet. He grabbed onto the shoulders of one of his thralls. He'd had too much to drink.

"This matter will be settled in the morning," he said as he turned and stumbled towards his chamber with the assistance of his thrall.

"This matter will be settled in the morning," Oleg said as he turned away to returned to sit with Thorn.

Rowan stood there looking at Oleg as he walked away.  He couldn't believe what just happened. Everyone else in the hall quietly watched on with amusement. It was clear to Rowan that most, if not all, of the people in this village seemed to now have a dislike for him in some form or another.

Rowan figured that it would be a good time to return the iron and items they brought back from the mound to the blacksmith's household.

He shoved his horn of mead into the hands of an idle thrall and walked out of the hall.

It was a relief to see that there was nobody outside, except a few villagers tending to their own business.  He'd had enough of the harassment for one day.

He bent down and began gathering up the iron bundles to carry.

"Do not listen to them," someone said, startling him.

It was Gwenda.

He lifted a bundle of iron, set it on his shoulder and then stood up to face her.

"I was just going to return this property back to

your household, my *lad-*."

He looked down without finishing what he was going to say.

"Sorry."

"Old habits," she said smiling at him. "It's going to take you some time getting used to not being a thrall any longer."

Rowan nodded.

"It will take them time as well, but they'll get used to it."

"I'm not so sure," he said while looking off in the distance at nothing in particular.

She knelt down, picked up the roll of chain mail and slung it over her shoulder.

Rowan gave her a puzzled look.

"Come on, I'll walk with you and help you carry this back."

"Thank you, my *la-*, erm,.. thank you. But are you sure you want to be seen with me?"

"I don't care about their gossip and grumbling. You earned your freedom and you earned your place among them. It was you that avenged my husband, not any of them. They have no place to complain."

Hearing her say this shocked Rowan and made him stop walking for a moment. Out of everyone upset about his emancipation, he thought she'd be the least happy of them all.

She looked back and smiled at him as she kept walking towards her family's longhouse.

Rowan smiled back and quickly caught up to her.

He wasn't used to being treated like this. It felt odd and he wasn't exactly sure how to act.

"So, Rowan the karl," she said. "Now that you are a karl, what do you plan to do with yourself?"

"What do you mean?"

"What do you plan to do with your life, now that you are a karl?"

"I haven't given it any real thought to be honest." he said. "It all happened so suddenly. I just never given it any thought."

"Why don't you stay with us for a little while until you get it sorted out," she offered. "We could use your help"

Rowan didn't immediately answer.

On one hand, he did need a place to stay where he wouldn't be constantly harassed. Some of the men in the jarl's hall just wouldn't let it go. Then on the other hand, this is the household of which he was a thrall. Would they see him as anything other than being their servant?

They approached the longhouse and Gwenda could sense Rowan's hesitancy

"Look," she said. "You don't have to answer right away. Sleep on it and give it some thought first. Please stay the night as our guest, Rowan."

"Thank you," he said as they approached the door to the Blacksmith's longhouse. A door he'd never passed through before as a freeman.

A part of him longed for things to be back how they were.

# Chapter 19

Following behind Gwenda, Rowan entered the household of his former master, the blacksmith. He immediately smelled the fresh baked bread and honey biscuits that Helga made.

She sat near the fire diligently spinning wool on a different distaff humming an old lullaby in some old and forgotten language. Nobody understood the words except Grandmother Helga.

She smiled at them as they sat the iron bundles down in the blacksmith area as they came in.

Nobody really knew how old Helga really was and Rowan remembered once hearing Gwenda confess to her husband that she wasn't really sure if Helga was her mother or grandmother.

Helga maintained many of her old habits and usually wore a scarf over her grayed hair, which she kept in a partially braided bun.

The smell of fresh bread wasn't the only thing permeating the air of the longhouse. Near the fire hung a haunch of mutton rubbed with dried sweet grasses and honey. It had been slowly smoking all day and mouth-watering aroma clung everywhere.

Directly over the fire hung a black iron kettle that had been fabricated years ago by her husband's father's father. A tribute to the durability of the skilled blacksmiths that had passed on their trade generation after generation.

They were said to be related to the original founders of the fjord's jarldom.

"Hello Rowan," said Thelsa who stood next to the kettle slowly stirring it.

"Please," Gwenda said, "sit in my husband's place as my guest."

She motioned for him to take a seat on the bench at the table where Bjord usually sat.

It felt strange when he sat down. He'd sat there before when nobody was looking, but it was different when he was allowed.

She walked over and picked up Bjord's battle ax that was sat leaning against the anvil stone.

"I want you to have my husband's ax as a personal reward for avenging his death."

270

She handed Rowan the ax.

He took it, not knowing what to say.

"He'd gotten it from a trader years ago when he got you. Maybe you and the ax belong together, I don't know. He never said.  I just know I want you to have it now."

"Thank you," he said as he set it down leaning against the bench.

Gwenda sat down and Thelsa brought them food and drink.

They spent most of the evening talking.

Rowan mostly listened as Gwenda explained her plans on how she was going to trade the blacksmithing items for cattle. It was how she was going to make end's meet now that Bjord was gone.

When they went to bed, Rowan slept restlessly throughout the night with strange dreams.

Once he dreamt that he was standing outside of the hollow where he hid after he escaped the draug and nearly fell to his death. He saw the Lady in the Forest walk up carrying a distaff. She placed it in the hollow and then walked away.  As he watched her fade away into the mist, he heard an infant crying from inside the hollow.

Rowan woke up to someone screaming.

It was Thelsa.

He quickly got up and out of his bedding.

"What is it?" he said.

"What's happened?" said Gwenda.

"The animals," Thelsa said. "They're dead."

"What?" Gwenda walked over to the barn where Thelsa was to look and was horrified at what she saw.

The cows, sheep, and even the geese all laid there on the ground dead.

"Where's grumpy?" Thelsa said as she started to look around for their goat. He was no where to be found, but that wasn't unusual with Grumpy.

She heard the goat bleating outside and said, "he's out here!" as she ran out the door.

They all went outside to investigate and found Grumpy outside perched on the steep of the longhouse's roof.

"How did he get up there," asked Helga.

"I don't know," Gwenda said.

Helga looked around and spotted Thorn walking up towards the longhouse.

"Here comes your late husband's brother."

"Hail Thorn," Thelsa called out to him.

"Hail Gwenda," he said as he walked up.

"Hail Helga, Thelsa." He looked at Rowan and then looked at Gwenda.

"Thorn," she said, "there is trouble in my house. Come see!"

She grabbed thorn by the hand and led him inside and showed him the livestock.

"It's that thrall," he said. "He has killed them as he's killed your husband and your own son. Why did you bring him back into your house?"

"That's nonsense," she said. "He's been in here with us the whole night. Plus look at them. There's no blood. It's as if they all just laid down and died."

"It's sorcery! Like that dead thing that came and killed your husband, my brother and your son, my nephew!"

"That creature did not come after my husband or my son and they weren't the only ones that it killed. It did not kill these animals, something else has. It looks like someone may have poisoned them. Which brings us to question why you're suddenly here."

"Don't test me woman -"

"Or what? The law has already proven this

property to be mine. How am I to know it was not you that poisoned our livestock in order to run us off so you can take possession of your deceased brother's blacksmithing house?"

"That is nonsense."

Their bickering was interrupted by the sound of Grumpy's demand that somebody get him off the roof expressed by a loud and annoying bleat.

Thorn went back outside to look at the goat on the longhouse's roof.

"How are we going to get him down?" asked Thelsa.

She was worried about her goat. She'd remained outside the whole time and kept an eye on him as he repeated his distaste at being on the roof.

"Someone will have to climb up there and tie a rope around him to lower him down," Thorn said. "It's the only thing I can think to do."

"I'll do it." offered Rowan.

"No," Thorn said. "I'll do it."

He did not want to go on the roof, but he didn't want Rowan to show him up and be the one that rescued the goat.

"Move aside," he said as he rudely pushed past

Rowan and climbed up the stack of firewood resting against the wall of the longhouse.

"Be careful Uncle Thorn," Thelsa said with a worried look.

"Don't worry sweetie, I'll get your goat."

It had rained some that night and everything was slick. Thorn nearly slipped on top of the logs as he stood on them to pull himself up on the roof.

The roof seemed steeper now it was wet. He crawled his way up with extreme care, being mindful of the thatching as to not go through the roof.

He got up on the steep and raised himself up to walk across the beam. The goat was standing there looking at him on the opposite end.

It bleated again, almost as if mocking.

Thorn carefully walked across the wet beam towards the goat.  As soon as he was within reach of it, the goat jumped past him onto the thatching.  It looked back at Thorn and bleated once more before hopping its way down onto the log pile and then onto the ground.

"Grumpy!" Thelsa ran and embraced the goat which just stood there and ignored her.

"Well, obviously the goat didn't need any help

getting down." Thorn said as he turned around and carefully began making his way back across the roof's steep.

As soon as he turned to lower himself down to crawl back down the thatching, he slipped on the damp wood and tumbled backwards.

Thorn fell backwards down the side of the roof, bouncing off of it four times before he finally hit the ground with a dull thud.

Gwenda ran to him.

Red-faced with anger and gasping for air, Thorn laid there on the ground with his arm oddly positioned under him.

Gwenda helped him sit up.

He cradled his arm and said, "I think I may have broken my arm."

Gwenda helped him up and called for her mother as she led him inside the longhouse.

"What's happened?" Helga said as she made her way towards the bench where Gwenda sat Thorn who was still cradling his arm.

"He fell off the roof and may have broken his arm."

"Pfffft, halfwit," snorted Helga, trying not to

laugh. "Let me have a look at it."

Thorn frowned at her and held up his arm. Helga took a look at it, prodding here and there.

"It doesn't appear to be broken," she said. "It may just be sprained, you will still have to put it in a sling."

"He also had a gash across his forearm," Gwenda said.

"Clean and bandage that so it doesn't fester. Put his flimsy arm in a sling to heal,"

Helga walked off shaking her head and sat down at the table.

Gwenda cleaned thorn's wound and then took some clean strips of linen and bound it. She reached over him to tie a sling around him and they locked eyes. They just froze and stared at each other in the eyes.

Then suddenly and unexpectedly they kissed.

It was long and deep kiss that came as a big surprise to everyone looking on, including the goat Grumpy who objected by letting out an annoying bleat.

"Well," Helga said. "That explains a lot."

There was an awkward silence as the two

embraced again and kissed even more passionately than before.

Rowan looked over at grandmother Helga, who just cocked her to the side and shrugged her shoulders.

Thelsa just stood there with her jaw half dropped in shock.

She didn't even notice Grumpy leaving her side as he pranced across the room and leapt up on top of the stone anvil.

For just a fraction of a second, Rowan thought he saw a twinkle in the goat's eye.

He did, however, notice something he'd never noticed about the goat before. It didn't have those weird rectangular pupils like other goats. This goat's eyes were different. They were almost like a person's pupils.

"Hello!?"

Somebody was at the door.

It was a short stout man with a very bushy beard. He stood outside at the open doorway holding the hood of his leather cloak over his head. It was beginning the rain again.

"I don't mean to disturb," he said apologetically. "But they call for Rowan at the jarl's hall."

"Do you know what it's about," asked Gwenda.

The man shook his head as he stepped back outside to wait.

Rowan stood up and gathered his things. His pack seemed a little bit heavier than it had been before. He picked up his small ax and tucked the handle in his belt and grabbed Bjord's ax.

"Run along thrall," Thorn said as Rowan walked outside. Gwenda scolded him for it.

Rowan paid him no mind as he walked out the door and accompanied the man to the jarl's hall.

His mind raced the entire walk as the rain pelted him at an angle making him cock his head to the side to prevent it from going into his ear.

# Chapter 20

"Here's the thrall now," announced Oleg the very moment Rowan walked into the jarl's hall. "Here comes the girly man that dares to insult me."

There was a small gathering of men already in the hall. Most stared at Rowan scornfully as he walked past them towards the jarl.

"I demand justice," he said.

"Alright now!" Jarl Erling said. "Enough of that."

Rowan stood before Jarl Erling. Alvis the Lawspeaker sat next to him and Auga sat on his other side.

"My honor was challenged and I was insulted," Oleg said.

"You will have a chance to speak as will the accused."

*"Accused?!"* Rowan thought in alarm.

"Rowan," said Jarl Erling to everyone in the hall as he stood up. "A dispute has been called to my attention."

Jarl Erling pointed at Oleg and said, "Oleg, before this hall and before our lawspeaker, state your complaint."

"I have been insulted by this thrall," said Oleg in voice loud enough for everyone in the hall to hear.

"I have warned you to stop insulting my house," said Jarl Erling. "He is no llonger a thrall and you know it.  I will hear no more of that."

"I have been insulted and I demand justice," Oleg restated.

"How did he insult you, Oleg?"

"He got hostile and got in my face," he said. "He challenged me and even went as far as putting his hand on the ax in his belt."

Jarl Erling rose an eyebrow and said, "you know that's a bogus claim, Oleg."

"Those who were in the hall heard him as did you, my lord." Oleg said. "You stated that this matter would be settled this morning."

Jarl Erling rolled his eyes and looked at Alvis.

"If he has been insulted, he does have a right to

holmgang to settle the matter," said Alvis, "according to our laws."

The Jarl let out a slow sigh.

"Rowan." he said. "It is claimed with witnesses that you insulted and challenged Oleg. Do you dispute this claim?"

Rowan stood quiet for a moment, unsure of what exactly was going on or what to say. Holmgang was a challenge to combat. It was a challenge to a duel to the death in order to settle a dispute. What dispute?

"Well?" the jarl said. "What do you have to say?"

"I did not insult this man," Rowan said, "it was he that insulted me."

"That is false!" Oleg said. "And now you insult me by lying! I demand justice settled in a manner to retain my honor."

"I do not lie," Rowan said. "I have no reason to lie."

"And now you say that I am a liar!" said Oleg.

"I said no such thing."

"You claim you are a karl, but are you really man enough to back your words like a karl?"

"Of course I back my words!" said Rowan, becoming angered and raising his voice.

"He bewitched the lands!" someone yelled from the back of the hall.

"His story doesn't add up about the draug," shouted another man. "Many people think he killed his master and made up the story," said someone.

"He caused the völva to die," said a man.

"This is true!" Oleg said. "He killed his master. He is no karl, he is a murderous thrall."

"Enough!" Jarl Erling said as he slammed his fist down on the arm of his chair and stood up.

"Fine!" he said. "We will forgo the customary waiting of a few days and settle it now!"

He turned and looked at Alvis, who nodded.

"Thralls!"

The hall grew quiet as three of the jarl's thralls scrambled through everyone to stand before him. Rowan's heart began to beat faster as he realized what just happened.

"Lay a cloak in the courtyard and stake it to the ground," he said.

He looked at the other two thralls and said, "you fetch two shields and you get two axes. Lay them on the cloak. Go now!"

They scurried off to do as the jarl as instructed

them.

Jarl Erling turned and addressed everyone in the hall.

"This matter will be resolved once and for all in the courtyard outside."

He turned and looked Auga directly in the eyes and said, "I hope this makes you happy."

"Everyone gather outside and make witness that this dispute is settled in a fair and honorable manner," he said before walking off.

# Chapter 21

Word traveled quickly and even though it was beginning to rain again, many folk were gathering to watch. Many of the men were making bets on the outcome.

Jarl Erling walked forward and made the announcement, although it clearly wasn't necessary. The whole village clearly were already aware.

"A dispute has been called to be settled by the tradition of holmgang. Both men will be stand on a island we have created with a cloak and they settle their dispute by means of combat."

The Jarl turned and pointed to a wool cloak that one of his thralls had spread out and staked to the ground at the ends.

"I have staked a cloak to the ground. This will be the island of which they will walk in combat. The fight begins the very instant both men have placed both of their feet on the cloak.  After which, both men will remain on the island and keep at least one foot on the cloak at all times until the contest has been decided. Two men will step on the island, but only one man leaves."

The jarl turned and looked at Rowan and said, "do you understand?"

Rowan nodded as one of the jarl's thralls handed him one of the shields and ax.

Jarl Erling turned and faced Oleg.

"Do you understand?"

Oleg nodded and tapped his shield twice with his ax as he planted both feet on the cloak pinned to the ground.

Rowan hesitated. He was no match for this man. He wasn't even trained, he'd only seen other men practicing. There was no way he could take on Oleg.

"Step onto the island," said Jarl Erling without making eye contact.

"See, what did I tell you. He's an honor-less coward," Oleg said as he raised his arms up to the approving grunts of some of the men watching.

He had to do this.  He had no choice.

The other men in the village will never let him be

if he did not prove himself right here and right now.

Determined, or foolhardy, Rowan stepped forward onto the cloak.

Before his other foot was all the way over, Oleg charged at him and slammed his shield into him. Rowan took a step to the right and pushed past him.

He heard Oleg's ax swish past his head when he did.

Rowan quickly turned around to face him with his shield up as Oleg charged again swinging his ax sideways as he did. Rowan brought his shield up and nearly lost grip of it from the force of Oleg's hit.

They both heard the shield crack from the hit.

Some of the men watching exchanged silver between themselves and made bets.

Oleg began to mock him by taking a few wild swings as they slowly circled each other on the cloak island.  Rowan was able to easily block them.

When Oleg faked a step to the left, he made Rowan flinch and block. This made Oleg laugh and start mocking him by thrusting his shield at Rowan a couple times while he made grunting sounds.

Rowan blocked and shoved them back with his shield until finally he took a wild swing with his ax at Oleg's face.

This made Oleg duck and take a step backward.

"Oooooh, she almost almost trimmed my beard like a good little thrall," he said with a laugh as he wiped some of the rain from his eyes with his arm.

The crowd watching laughed with him.

Rowan charged forward trying to shove Oleg back as he angrily swung his ax again, but Oleg brushed it aside with his shield.

"Oh no," he mocked, "I think I made her angry."

The crowd laughed harder when Rowan almost slipped on the wet cloak.  Some of the onlookers increased their bets.

Rowan charged at him again and tried to knock him off balance by shoving into him with his shield. But Oleg was too strong for any of that and shoved him back two steps. He almost stepped off the cloak into the mud when he went back.

Oleg charged at him again and Rowan was able to once again slide past him, but he lost grip of his shield when Oleg clipped it with his ax and pulled it out of his hand.

He quickly ducked Oleg's swing and tried to slide past him but Oleg managed to trip him when he did.

Rowan fell face fist to the ground and dropped

his ax.

He looked back and saw Oleg bringing his ax down and rolled out of the way.

When Oleg took another swing at him, he rolled towards his ax and picked it up as he scrambled to his feet.  He spun away from the next swing and felt the swish of the ax nearly slice across his face.

He swung at him once again, but this time Rowan swung his ax down trying to block it and hit him in the wrist.

Oleg howled out in pain as he dropped his ax and flung his shield at Rowan.

Rowan tried to dodge Oleg's shield but was clipped in the face when he tried to duck. The hit gave him a black eye and a small gash that ran from his left eye brow down to his cheek.

Oleg dropped to his knees holding his bloodied wrist and roared out again in pain.

Rowan knew it was his only chance and grasp the ax with both hands and swung at Oleg's head. His swing came up short and too low, but he did manage to clip Oleg in the throat and slice it open.

The cheers and taunts from the men watching suddenly stopped and the rain could be heard pelting the ground as Oleg choked.

Blood streamed down from under his beard and ran across his chest with the rain. He had a look of surprise in his eyes and tried to speak, but only spat out blood.

Oleg fell dead to the ground.

After a moment, Jarl Erling walked over past the grumbling men and knelt down beside Oleg. He rolled him on his side and looked at him before rolling him back and standing up.

"Oleg is dead and has lost this dispute," he announced. "Rowan has won and holds his honor. This matter is now settled."

He turned to return to his hall before a man boldly stepped in front of him and said, "and what about the weregeld?"

Jarl Erling briefly looked the man up and down before he finally said, "he was challenged to holmgang and won. He owes no weregeld in this matter."

"He owes the family a weregeld." demanded the man.

"He owes no weregeld." repeated the Jarl, staring the man down.

The man stepped closer and got in the Jarl's face.

"He owes-"

Before the man could finish his words, the jarl drew a knife from his belt and stabbed the man in the chest.

With his free hand, he grabbed him by the shoulder and drove his knife in even deeper.

The man tried to pull out his ax from his belt, but dropped it on the ground. His arms went limp when Jarl Erling forcefully pulled his knife out from his chest. He stared blankly in the air as the jarl stabbed him again.

The jarl let go of him and took a step back.

The man looked down at the blood spilling from his chest and then looked up at the jarl and tried to speak, but fell to his side and died.

"Does anyone else question my rule in these lands?" said the jarl as he turned towards the crowd of shocked onlookers, still holding the bloodied knife in his hand.

The moment was broken when by a crackle of thunder announced a flash of lightning in the sky which was immediately followed by someone near the docks yelling, "longship!"

Everyone turned and looked down past the docks through the haze of the rain and saw a longship on the fjord oaring its way towards the harbor.

This ship didn't come to trade. It was a viking longship of war.

"Damn the gods!" Jarl Erling snarled under his breath as he turned and walked through the crowd towards his hall.

Jarl Erling knew what this ship wanted and he was not happy about it.

"What is it my love?" Auga asked as she followed behind him inside the mead hall.

"The longship," he said. "It's either coming to call for men to go to battle or it's here to call men to go viking."

"What's wrong with that?" she asked.

"Men and ships that leave to go viking never come back. I've allowed a couple ships to leave once before and they never returned."

"I see," she said. "I had no idea."

"And men sent to war never return as well," he said. "The timing for this ship's arrival couldn't come at a worse time."

"My love," she said, "what about Rowan?"

"What about Rowan? That matter has just been settled outside. Apparently your plan failed."

"No my love, it's an opportunity to be rid of him."

294

"Be rid if him? He has done nothing wrong."

He turned and took her by the shoulders, looked
her in the eyes and said, "you're not falling for that
superstitious gossip too, are you?"

"No, I was actually thinking about his welfare
actually," she said coyly. "There are many in this
village that do believe that he is the cause of their
problems and these accusations and these challenges
and holmgangs are just going to continue until
someone finally kills him."

"He's not the cause of what's been happening to
this village," he said quietly to himself.

"What?"

"Nothing. He's the one who inadvertently helped
put a stop to it."

"Yes my love, but there still are many that remain
bitter over him. Perhaps this ship offers an
opportunity to send him away and let the folk of this
village put all these recent events behind them."

He looked at her without expression.

She was right. He didn't even know this thrall's
name or even care until all this started happening in
his village. The whole thing made many of his men
question his authority.  It would be better to send
him away and let things go back to where they were

before.

"You are right, my dear," he said as he turned and sat in his chair.

A housekarl burst into the hall, "My lord! A man has come with a bidding stick calling for men to come to Odin!"

The Jarl immediately stood up.

"What does that mean?" said Auga.

"It's a call for men to go to battle," he said as he made his way through the hall and went out the door.

Besides the folk that had come to witness the duel, more people were coming as word about the longship's arrival spread. Even some thralls took a break from their toils to see what the commotion was all about at the harbor.

"O-DIN!" called out a middle-aged man clad in chain mail with a brown bear skin draped over his shoulder. The curls of his long grayed hair came out from the spangenhelm he wore on his head.

He was carrying a long spear which had its head dipped in pitch and was lit aflame.  He held it up in the air as he walked towards the jarl's hall from the docks below.

"ODIN!" he called out again.

The man periodically called out the god of war, Odin at the top of his lungs every few steps as he walked up the trail towards the jarl's hall.

Jarl Erling met the man before he came in front of the hall.

"Hail messenger!" he said. "Welcome to my hall!"

The man stopped and grabbed the spear he was carrying with both hands and planted it into the muddy ground. The pitch dipped iron spearhead continued to burn for all could see.

Satisfied that the spear was securely planted, the man stepped back, pulled off his helm and called out again.

"ODIN!"

"Thank you for your welcome, Jarl Erling!" the man said. "I am Huthar."

"Welcome Huthar!" said Jarl Erling.

"I have come to call men to Odin! The gods call for those brave and worthy to the lands south of the sea in Juteland. The fires of a great battle are burning and our brethren to the south call for men to join them for a chance that Odin will favor them the lands of their enemies or give them a place of honor with him in his halls."

"We heed your call, Huthar." said Jarl Erling.

"Come and refresh yourself in my hall as my guest!"

"You are most gracious and I thank you for your hospitality," he said. "But I only have time to gather fresh water and men and then I must be off."

Huthar made his announcement again two more times at the gathering crowd before he removed the spear and walked back towards the docks.

There were a few men who were gathering their things to take him up on the offer.

Rowan rinsed the gash near his eye in a puddle and someone threw a clump of mud at him as he did. He turned to see who had done it but could not tell who it was, although there were a few people laughing.

He began to walk back towards the jarl's hall when someone threw mud at him again and hit him in the back of the head.

There was a small stone in the mud and Rowan's head rang for the hit.

Again nobody claimed responsibility.

Jarl Erling noticed and called Rowan over to him.

"Look," he said to Rowan, "this is an opportunity for you. This harassment will never stop. Take this opportunity and get aboard that longship and start a new life with your freedom."

Rowan wiped the mud from the back of his head and nodded.

He really had nowhere to go and he wasn't going to be accepted here any longer.

It was time for him to go.

# Chapter 22

Rowan took his place with the rest of the men aboard the longship who were answering the call of Odin.

Nobody said a hardly a word towards each other as they made way. The rain had cleared and the sun was beginning to warm the day.

He brought with him, the ax of Bjord's that had been given to him by Gwenda and the smaller ax he carried in his belt.  Jarl Erling had also given him a new shield when he gathered up his things to leave. The jarl had been very kind to him, but it was time for Rowan to leave.

This was a call for warriors to go into battle with the promise of lands to be settled by the victors. It couldn't have come at a better time for Rowan.  He, as did many other men, had no where else to go and could no longer stay where they were.

There were no other options.

The shield Jarl Erling gave him was unpainted with leather stretched over it.  It was one of the better shields that the jarl's own Housekarl Guard personally carried.  He would have to decide how to paint it.

He would also have to learn how to use it properly too.

Along with his pack, he stowed everything in a nice bundle under the bench he sat. He was given a place on the ship to row with the other men.

Some of the other men tended to the ship's ropes when they cast off as an older and more seasoned man leaned on the tiller as everyone else pulled on the oars.

Rowan looked back at the hill coming down into the waters as he steadily rowed with the other men. He could see the thick smoke of a pyre bellowing high into the air near the blacksmith's longhouse. They were burning the livestock that had mysteriously died in the night.

He could also see someone herding some cattle towards the longhouse.

*"It must be Thorn," Rowan thought. "He's probably moving in."*

There was a peaceful calm to the fjord.

With barely any wind, the men kept to the oars. The man called Huthar, who summoned the men, tapped a steady beat on the ship's floor boards with the end of a spear to keep the men in rhythm as they rowed.

They rowed for hours and periodically, he would call out for everyone to switch sides or to take a short break.

Being aboard the ship reminded Rowan of the trip he'd taken across the seas when he was a small boy. It was after his village had been attacked and a trader found him hidden in the burnt ruins of his family's longhouse.

The trader put him aboard a knarr boat and they sailed across the cold waters of the sea towards the mountainous lands of the north. Their boat fought across a violent and angry sea as it sailed on. The trading vessel crashed over savage waves as the wind howled beyond the darkness.

Rowan held on for dear life with wide eyes as the men aboard the ship laughed at the angry sea and mocked it.

The trader tied Rowan to the mast and said, "don't worry boy, the gods aren't coming for you today!"

When the sea calmed and the morning mist lifted, Rowan could see that they were sailing along steep bluffs. They followed the bluffs until they finally entered the pristine fjords which led to the harbor where he was sold to the blacksmith.

The very fjords they were leaving now.

The man at the tiller saw some longships coming in the opposite direction ahead of them and immediately stood up from his bench to get a better look.

"Longships!" he called out while pointing.

Everyone stopped rowing and turned to look. Some of the men stood up from their benches to see better.

There were three longships steadily rowing ahead of them on the opposite side of the fjord.

"Let us be ready for anything if they turn towards us!" Huthar said. "Otherwise let us have nothing to do with them."

They all sat back down and began rowing their longship once again, except Huthar who kept a keen eye on them as they went.

The ships did turn towards them.

"They're turning toward us," he said, "make yourselves ready for battle.  I will light the bidding stick so they know we are not to be attacked. I cannot guarantee they'll honor it."

Huthar lit the pitch on the end of the long spear he used as a bidding stick when he gathered the men and held it up high while he stood at the forecastle.

There was no way the other longships approaching could not see it.

After a few moments, two of the other longships veered back on their original course, but one continued to advance towards them.

"One's still coming," said one of the men rowing.

"Yes, it looks like it," Huthar said as he dosed the bidding stick in the splashing waves. "Secure the oars and ready yourselves!"

"It looks like they want to die," he said as he tossed the long spear on the deck.

Huthar turned and looked back at the approaching longship and studied it for a moment.

"There's a chance we can blow past them," he said. "If we can push past them, they will not be able to turn around quick enough to give pursuit."

"So what do we do?" a man asked.

"Get ready for a fight if this does not work," he said, looking each man in the eye to make sure they understood what he meant. "Otherwise take the oars men and row your hearts out!"

There was a roar of acknowledgment as the men at the oars began to row vigorously.

"When they get close, I want you to steer away from them as much as possible," he instructed the man on the tiller.

"If they come to our side, make sure you pull your oars in so they don't sheer them in half!" he said to the rest of the men at the oars.

He watched the approaching longship for a moment and then said, "I want the men on the front bench to pull your oars in and take arms!"

Huthar put on his sword belt and fastened it.

"You two men with bows," he said, "pull your oars in and put some arrows into them! Send them to Valhalla!"

They pulled their oar in and scrambled to grab their bows.

The men in front armed and readied themselves with their shields, while the two men notched their arrows and drew their strings.

"After we pull our oars in, grab your shield and ax as fast as you can. They will try to rush us," said the man rowing next to Rowan.

306

Rowan nodded as he kept pace rowing with the other men.

"I only see one archer," Huthar said. "Take him out!"

The two bowmen began to release their arrows at the men in the approaching longship while the archer on the other longship fired back.

An arrow struck one of the bowmen in the leg just as his arrow hit the opposing archer in the arm with one of his arrows.

"Steer hard right!" Huthar said as he grabbed a hold of one of the mast's ropes. "Brace yourselves!"

The longships slammed together bow to bow on their port sides. The force caused the longships to careen slightly as the men on both sides tumbled uncontrollably forward onto the decks.

The men on the other ship threw grappling irons at Huthar's longship to secure it to theirs and began to leap aboard and attack.

Huthar had not yet put on his helm, but drew his sword and leapt at once on the forecastle at the men that had come on his longship.

Upon landing, he struck one man his death-blow with his sword by cutting him down from shoulder to chest.

A man on the other longship hurled a spear at
Huthar and nearly struck him in the waist. Huthar
saw it coming in the corner of his eye and managed
to turned away quick enough to dodge it.  The spear
flew past him and hit the man behind him in the
foot, causing him to cry out in pain.

Huthar turned and grabbed the shaft of the spear
that had pierced through the man's foot and stuck in
the deck.

"Get ready to scream!" he said to the man as he
pulled the spear loose.

The man cried out in agony.

Huthar turned and threw the spear back at the
man who'd thrown it at him and killed him where he
stood.

Rowan picked himself up from being tumbled
over his oar and reached down to pick up his shield.
Just as he grabbed it, an arrow struck next to his
hand and knocked it out of his grip.

He picked the shield back up and broke the
arrow shaft off.

Huthar pulled his sword free from the man he'd
nearly cut in half using his foot to push the man
back.

"Cut the ropes!" he yelled as he charged forward

at the other men who'd come aboard. He swung
with his sword and hit one man in the shield while
hitting another shield on his back swing.

Huthar swung at them again against their raised
shields and charged forward at them like a bull and
shoved them backwards.

One of the men with the spear was swift to seize
the moment and stabbed one to death as he fell on
his back and dropped his shield.

Huthar reached down and picked up the man's
shield and turned towards the other man who was
already thrusting his sword at Huthar. He was able
to get the shield up in time to catch the blow which
struck into the shield and cut him on the arm.

He roared and gave the shield a twist with the
sword pierced in it and broke it short off at the hilt.
The stunned man drew back just as Huthar swung at
him with his sword and sliced him from armpit to
armpit.

Rowan had his shield and ax ready, but the other
men attacking had stopped leaping over. He noticed
one of the grappling hooks and stepped over the oar
to get to it. An arrow flew past his face and struck
the man who'd been at the oar next to him in the
chest. He slumped down to his knees and fell
forward dead.

Rowan chopped the rope with his ax and released the remaining grappling iron that kept the two longships tethered.

The longships began to pull apart as the remaining crew on the attacking longship took to the oars and scrambled to make way.

One man tried to leap back to his ship, but Huthar cut both his legs from under him while he leapt, causing him to fall short and tumble in the cold waters of the fjord.

"Take to the oars!" Huthar yelled.

The men aboard scrambled to get back to their positions on the oars.  Rowan looked over the side and saw the man who'd been cut down drift past. Rowan could see his eyes looking back at him and felt bad for the man. That is, until he heard an arrow strike the side of the hull near him.

Defiant to the end, one of the men on the other longship had picked up the bow from the wounded archer and was firing at them.

"The oars!" Huthar said. "Row men, row!"

Huthar also took a bench and began rowing as he encouraged the other men.

Rowan sat down, shoved the oar out and began rowing with the other men.  He saw blood on his hand and remembered the arrow that knocked the shield out of his hand.

"They're turning back!" said the man at the tiller.

"Keep rowing," said Huthar. "If we pick up speed they'll never be able to catch up."

The men pulled on the oars until the longship began to glide across the fjord once again. They stayed well ahead of the other longship until it finally gave up chase and turned.

"The wind has come back," said a man rowing.

"Yes it has," said Huthar. "The gods have taken favor on us. Let us use the wind and part ways from these hostile waters."

The men aboard were relieved to have the winds back and pulled their oars in as the sail was hoisted. The wind quickly filled their sail and they were now soaring across the waves.

They were able to reach the open sea before nightfall.

Once out in the open sea, the experience of Huthar and cooperative winds carried them steadfast to their destinaton.

# Chapter 23

As the men aboard Huthar's longship came closer to land, they could see the fires of many camps along the shore. They used the lights to guide them in closer until the sun rose and led them to the long port where they docked.

There were many other men disembarking from different longships that came from every corner of the northern world.

Casting off, Huthar bid them a farewell and instructed them where to go.

"Follow the path of tall stakes with reindeer antlers tied on top of them. These stakes lead to where the different tribes have set up their tents looking for men to join them.  The tents will be marked with tall burning bidding spears in front of them. Don't worry, you won't miss them. There are many of them," he said.

There were tents and huts everywhere.

Some of the tents were from linen cloth, while others were made of leather or hide.  Most of the makeshift huts were made from weaved sticks and thatching and then covered in moss.

They were enough to keep the head's dry of the inhabitants inside but not much else.

Rowan was aimlessly following the stakes with a few of the other men when a rather robust man stepped in front of him and blocked his way.

"I am Olvar," the man said. "I have been waiting for you."

"Waiting for me?"

"Are you the one called Rowan?"

"Yes, I am called Rowan."

"I have been waiting on you," said Olvar. "I have been sent to prepare you for battle."

"Prepare me for battle?" asked Rowan puzzled. "You were sent by whom?"

"A trader," said Olvar. "He paid me in silver and told me to watch for a scrawny boy with a thrall's haircut coming from the North to join the tribes in battle."

Rowan was speechless with a confused look on

his face. Who is this trader and why has he paid this man to train him?

Olvar stood there with a warm smile beaming from from his rough weather beaten warrior's face.

He was a huge man with a bear skin cloak draped over his shoulders. His amber and white hair was gathered and wound into a single knot on the side of his head.  There were white stripes streaking down his bushy beard that was as orange as the sun.

"Are you ready to learn how to defend yourself in combat, young Rowan?" Olvar said.

Before Rowan could answer, Olvar slammed into him with his shoulder and slapped him under the leg.

Rowan flew backwards in the air and hit his head on a rock as he landed.

He was out cold.

~

Rowan woke up to water being dumped on him. He gasped and flung his arms about as he quickly fumbled to sit up.

"Sorry about that," Olvar said apologetically. "I should have looked to make sure it was safe behind you before introducing you to the art of glima."

He offered him a cup of fresh water.

Rowan took the cup and rubbed the back of his head.

"Yeah, you bumped your head pretty hard. Here take some of these." Olvar said, handing him some strips of white willow bark.

"It's from the bark of the white willow tree. Some of my grandmother's medicine, just chew on them."

"Come," he said, "let's get you settled. I have a shelter for us just over there."

Rowan took Olvar's extended hand and pulled himself up.

"You can put your stuff over there and we can get started," Olvar said as he led the way. "That is, if your head is up to it."

"I'll be fine," Rowan said as he followed him. "Get started?"

"Here it is." Olvar said pointing at a thatch hut. "It's nothing fancy, but it will keep the rain off your head."

Rowan put his things in the hut and when he came back out, Olvar handed him a chopping ax.

"You will get two things from that ax," Olvar said. "The first thing you will get is stronger."

"What is the second thing," Rowan asked as he watched Olvar walk away.

"Firewood for tonight."

Rowan spent much of his time chopping wood. He was either cutting down trees, cutting them into lengths, or splitting them. Olvar had him chopping wood in every direction in order to strengthen his arms and improve the accuracy of his swings.

Olvar also made him carry heavy stones from one pile to another. He would unstack one pile of stones and then re-stack them in another spot. Once done, he'd then stack them back in their original pile.

There were other young men doing the same thing and often unstacking and stacking the stones along side of him.

He went through a daily tedious cycle of manual labor to build his strength and stamina.

They also trained several times a day with weapons and shields.

Olvar taught Rowan different ways to use his shield. Both defensively and as a weapon. They also trained and practiced with the other men in formations. They practiced the shield wall against each other and they practiced the shield wall used against archers.

Rowan also learned about different weapons and how to use them. Olvar would take him around different parts of camps where there were weapons brought over from cultures far and away.

There were one trader who had a cart full of small clay pots he'd brought from the far east.

"They call them thunder balls," he explained. "You use them to confuse and scatter the enemy."

"How so," asked Rowan, now curious.

"You light the stem with fire and throw them at the enemy," said the trader. "They make a loud noise and puff of fire and smoke."

"Do they hurt them," asked Olvar looking at one closely.

"No," said the man. "They don't do much but scare. The armies to the east throw them over their enemy's line to confuse them when they attack."

"So they are just useless toys," Olvar said as he handed the small clay pot back to the man and walked off.

"Where did you get them," asked Rowan, still curious.

"They got them from the people of the eastern river who got them from nomad traders that came from the far east."

He picked one up out of the small pile and tossed it to Rowan who was starting to walk away and catch up to Olvar.

"Here, you can use one to scare one of your friends. Just don't throw it too close to them, they do make a loud fire. If you like them then you come back and I have many more to trade."

Rowan examined the ceramic ball. It was a sort small pot with a small opening stuffed with clay. There was a cord sticking out from the clay closing the opening. It wasn't very big, but felt solid. He stuffed it in his pack.

Later that day Rowan sat alone in their small hut with the small house cat that had moved in with them for the last couple of weeks.

He sat in the chair that was in the hut near the fire hearth and began unpacking his pack. He pulled out the strange ball made from pottery the man had given him.

The man had called it a 'thunder ball.'

Rowan wasn't sure exactly how this thing could have a burst of fire in it, much less sound like thunder. It didn't look possible to Rowan. He looked at it closely and tried to figure out how it could possibly make a loud noise to scare someone in battle.

He sat in his chair with the cat in the corner looking on intently as he contemplated how this ceramic ball could possibly work. He was now starting to think that he really needed to try this thing out on a flesh and blood moving target.

He wanted see if it really worked.

For a fraction of a second he did think about lighting it and tossing it by the cat, but thought better of it. She seemed like such a sweet cat and there was no reason for him to be mean and spook it.

Rowan sat there in the chair looking at this ceramic ball that was no bigger than a man's fist.

The cat looked on with her head cocked to one side as if to say, 'don't do it stupid.'

*"It's such a tiny lil ole thing, it couldn't be all that bad," he thought.*

He decided to light it and see what it did.

He took a small burning twig out of the fire and lit the cord sticking out of the so called 'thunder-ball.'

"We shall see what this little toy from the far east does," Rowan said to the cat.

He watched the cord catch fire and then sparkle as it burned its down to where it was packed into the ceramic ball.

320

A second after the cord burned into the ball, there was a short fizz and a small gray puff of smoke that came out of the hole.

*"That's it?"*

Rowan was disappointed and tossed it in the corner of the room.

*"Olvar was right," he thought. "A useless toy."*

He turned to reach in his bag again and..

BOOM… !!!

Rowan was pretty sure the thunder god himself had ran in there and picked him up in the chair he was sitting in and then body slammed them both, him still in the chair, on the ground.

He woke up on his side in the fetal position with tears in his eyes, body soaking wet, testicles nowhere to be found, and his left arm tucked under his body in the oddest position. There was also a weird tingling in his legs!

The cat was making meowing sounds he'd never heard before.  It was clinching for dear life to the wall thatch, obviously in an attempt to avoid getting slammed by his body as it flopped across the room.

He collected what little of his wits he had left and sat up to survey the situation.

His hair and forming beard were smoking at the tips.

The chair was flipped upside down on the other side of the hut.

His face felt like it had been slammed with a shield and his bottom lip was swollen. It felt like it weighed as heavy as a stone. He seemed to have no control of drooling at the moment.

Other men in the camp to came running to see what happened after they heard the sound.

A cloud of smoke rolled out of the wood thatch hut as Rowan pushed aside the door cover and stepped outside. The cat bolted out past his legs and disappeared into the darkness.

"What happened?" someone asked.

"Thu-dah bah." Rowan tried to say through his still tingling swollen lips.

"What?!" asked the man.

"Thuh-duh bah," Rowan tried to say.

"I still don't get -"

"Thunder Ball!" said one man as he started laughing.

Some of the other men started laughing as well.

Luckily, only Rowan's pride was hurt.  Olvar didn't say anything about it, except to tell him to stop playing with fire.

The swelling in his lip went down in a couple days. However, the cat never did return.

# Chapter 24

Rowan woke up to someone standing over him kicking his feet.

It was Olvar.

"Wake up little brother! Today's the day you may get the honor of meeting Odin himself!"

Rowan sat up and rubbed the sleep from his eyes.

"We're to march south and gather," Olvar said. The day has come, gather your things."

"I thought we had weeks until they came."

Olvar looked up towards the sky and said, "I was hoping to teach you to better use a sword, but it seems the gods are impatient to see a battle. They have decided that it is time to fill some of the benches in Valhalla."

He looked down at Rowan and said, "grab your things, it will take several hours for us to get there."

Olvar walked off and Rowan began gathering his things from inside the hut.

He took one last look around to make sure that he grabbed everything and took note that the cat still had not returned.

He walked over to where Olvar was standing with some other men and together they began walking. They went south with the other groups of men. Some of the groups were of entire families.

Olvar noticed him looking at a family that was walking near them.

"Yes, most of the warriors that have come to fight hope to reclaim their lands. They have no where else to go. They either win or starve by winter."

Olvar took a bite from a hunk of cheese he had tucked in his tunic and passed it over to a child walking next to them. The girl's eyes brighten as she took two quick bites and then handed it to her mother.

"Where do they all come from?" asked Rowan.

"Everywhere," said Olvar. "Most are northmen that have come because there is nothing for them in their homelands. Also, many of the tribes and families you see here have been pushed out of their homelands by the Karling."

"The Karling?"

"He claims to be the King of all freemen and he brings his armies of the Christ."

"What is the Christ?"

"Their god," Olvar said as he stopped walking. "Don't worry, their god is already dead. Not like Thor who's alive and kicking.

Olvar looked up at the sky and said, "And by the clouds forming, I'd say he's excited about the coming battle."

They walked a bit more as the morning sun slowly rose. When they came to an encampment, Rowan could see the smoke of many fires mixing with the early morning mists that clung to the bottom of the hill.

"We're here." said one of the men walking with them. "We are to go to the wood-line near the top of the hill.  That is where they are forming."

Olvar nodded to the man.

They walked with the other men as they moved through the encampment towards the crest of the hill.

People were scattered everywhere as men walked up the hill past them.

There was a group of people gathered around some women who were singing in a semi trace as they beat their drums.

One of the men pointed at a line of bound men that were being led up to a platform.

"They were captured last night by scouts," he said. "It's how we know they're coming today."

The drumming became more frantic and they all turned to watch what was going on.

The women took the prisoner ahead in the line and led him up a platform that was over a huge brazen cauldron. Some of the women crowned him with wreaths as he passed by them.

They raised him up and bend him over the cauldron. A bare foot gray haired old woman stood on the raised platform and began chanting.  She too was clad in all white, except for the pale yellow fur cloak that she wore.

The other women stopped tapping on their drums and chanted with her.

The old woman took a sword and cut the throat of the man they bent over the cauldron. His blood poured out into the huge cauldron.  A few of the women collected some of it in smaller vessels.

When the blood flow from his throat slowed,

they pulled him and some of the other women began to cut at his body. They spilled his entrails on the ground and began divining with it.

There was a look of horror on Rowan's face, along with some of the other men.

One of the older men laughed and said, "Don't worry boys, they're our witches. They sacrifice the men to the gods and use the blood to share the gods blessing upon us. They use the man's entrails to foretell the results of the battle."

"I hope their predictions are good," said a man who was leaning on his spear watching.

"Don't worry little brother, they're on our side." Olvar said. "And that's a good thing."

Rowan nodded.

They began walking through the encampment to reach the wood line over the crest. The rest of the men who stopped to watch the spectacle, turned and began walking too. They too, had seen enough.

On top of the hill, someone blew a horn.

Several others along the hill crest blew their horns too.

Olvar stopped walking and looked at Rowan.

"It is time," he said as he set his pack down.

"Leave your things here and dress for battle."

"What do you mean?" asked Rowan, puzzled as he set his things down on the ground.

A woman dressed in white walked up to him and dripped a bundle of twigs she had lashed together into a small urn and then spattered Rowan across the face and chest with it.

She dipped it again and splattered Olvar then another man standing next to him before walking off to another group of men and began splattering them.

Rowan looked at the red splatter across the other men and then looked down at the dripping red splatter across his chest.

"The gods will favor you now," Olvar said. "The enemy has arrived. It is time for battle."

Rowan put on a thick leather tunic and tied its lashings. He picked up the spangenhelm he got from a trader and adjusted the fur lining he stuck inside to make it fit his head better. It was a little big on him.

"You should have spent more silver and got the one with the visor to protect your face," Olvar said as he put his full visor spangenhelm on and tied the lashings underneath.

Rowan picked up his shield and grabbed his ax and spear as he waited for Olvar to finish lashing his

330

chain mail.

They walked over the crest and joined the lines of men forming. There were many tribes of north men and were many more that Rowan did not recognize.

All were side by side as he took his place among them just as they started yelling out across the battlefield.

The men of the Karling were forming their lines on the other side of the field. They had round shields and didn't look much different than they did, except for the robed men carrying huge crosses.

It looked like they were all carrying spears.

Rowan could see horsemen coming up from behind them. There was one horsemen with other men riding around him. One of them held a purple banner with white stars high in the air.

*"That must be their king," thought Rowan. "The one they call the Karling."*

He seen more horsemen ride up from the crest and join the others. They all wore helmets and had shields. Each horseman was also carrying a lance.

Rowan's heart sank and he watched them form their lines at the edge of the battlefield. The men on foot also continued to line up and form a long shield wall. There was so many of them.

The women who'd come with their men began to wail and plead for the men to not break their shield wall and let the enemy through.

"They will kill us all," they cried out. "Your children will become their slaves! They will rape and kill us all. Don't let them enslave our children!"

This did absolutely nothing for Rowan's already wrecked nerves.

Behind them he heard them beating on the hide drum skins they had stretched over wicker wagons they were pulling over the ridge. The drums made an unearthly sound that was terrifying and made Rowan's skin crawl.

The shields of the Karlings formed long lines and there were lines of men behind them.

Suddenly horns started blaring from the Karling side and he saw them marching forward to the beat of a drum. The men on horses formed on the far side of them, also moved forward at the same pace.

The men on Rowan's line began shouting and holding their spears up in the air.

He watched them slowly march closer and closer until he heard their horns blare again and they stopped marching forward. Their men stood side by side with their shields interlocked into a wall.

The men on Rowan's side continued to yell obscenities at them and dare them to come closer.

He heard their horns sound again and suddenly Rowan saw the thick cluster of dark lines suddenly come up from behind the enemy's line and climb the sky towards them.

He immediately knew what it was, arrows.

"Shield Wall!" someone yelled.

"Interlock your shields!"

Rowan lifted his shield up and took half a step forward like Olvar taught him. He held his shield up in the gap of the shields of the men in front of him. The men behind him held up their shields above his.

The arrows hit hard and it surprised Rowan. He didn't expect it them to hit so hard. One of the arrows struck his shield and penetrated halfway through.  It missed his arm by a hand's length.

His heart began to pound as he felt sweat start to roll down the side of his face. He was starting to get worried.

The arrows kept coming and another struck his shield and went through almost as far as the previous one had. Rowan looked at the arrow head nervously. It looked very sharp.

"Don't sweat those," he heard Olvar say behind

him. "When they stop pissing on us, just break those off like I showed you and be ready for whatever comes next."

Another arrow struck above where the previous one had, but penetrated further and almost hit Rowan in the eye.

He heard Olvar laughing behind him.

"I told you to try to get a helmet with a visor on it if you could afford it," he said.

Rowan wished he had spent the extra silver now.

He held firm and kept his shield up. The arrows were starting to become fewer, but he wasn't going to chance peeking through the gap to see if they were done yet.

Rowan felt the ground trembling and heard horns blaring from both sides. He didn't know what was going on. Except that his heart was racing.

"Shield Wall! Put your spears out!"

Rowan lowered his shield to brace the man in front of him and saw a line of men on horses galloping towards them with their lances down.

"Spears Forward!"

The horsemen were on them almost immediately. They braced for the impact behind their shields as they raised their spears.

Some horsemen crashed through and came over the men in front of him. They charged through and Rowan was knocked backwards by a horse as the man next to him was lanced.

The horse kicked him in the chest as he hit the ground and knocked the breath out of him.  It took a second for him to realize what just happened as he quickly sat up and grabbed his spear.

The shaft was broke in half.  It was useless. He tossed it aside.

The Karling's army had made it up to their lines and were now trying to push them back. Rowan grabbed his ax and stood up to join the fight but was hit hard from behind.

His helmet went flying off as he was slammed to the ground. His breath had been knocked out of him again and this time chocked when he tried to breathe. He rolled over and seen a horse reared up over him.

It was one of the Karling horsemen. Rowan rolled away just as it brought its hooves down.

He looked up and saw Olvar spearing the horsemen from behind just before the horse kicked him in the face.

The world went black.

# Chapter 25

Rowan woke to find himself covered in blankets, laying on sheep skin bedding. His body ached and it hurt too much move. He was able to raise his head enough to see that he was in a tent with an older warrior.

It was Olvar.

He'd seen him go down protecting him.  He was glad to see him in the tent. It meant he was alive.

The both of them were seriously injured from the battle and were having their wounds tended to by some women in the camp.

Olvar had been wounded by a spear to his chest; so he had to be set up in his bedding for about an hour each afternoon to help drain the fluids from his lungs.

It saddened Rowan to hear his weak raspy cough, but he could tell it helped his breathing.

Olvar's bedding was next to the tent's only opening, so he was able to see the world outside.

Rowan was forced to spend all of his time recovering by laying flat on his back. The bandaging on his forehead prevented him from seeing much anyways. When he wasn't drifting off to sleep or being tended to by one of the camp's women, he was staring at his grand view of the tent's ceiling.

Rowan and Olvar talked for hours on end to pass the time away.

Olvar spoke of his wife and of his infant son when he was a younger man. He spoke about how he'd lost them after his village had been attacked and he was forced to flee without them. He told Rowan about his old home then and when he was a blacksmith.

Rowan told him about the draug on the mound and of his escape.

Olvar didn't believe him.

He would tell Rowan of previous battles that he'd been in and of the times he'd been on viking adventures along the coast of West Francia.

It became routine, every afternoon when Olvar would be propped up in his bed by the tent opening to drain the fluids from his lungs, that he'd pass the time by describing all the things he could see outside the tent opening to Rowan.

Rowan began to live for those short periods where his world would be broadened and enlivened by all the activity and color of the world outside, described to him by Olvar.

The tent's opening overlooked a meadow with a lovely lake.

Ducks and swans swam on the water while children played in the fields. Olvar told Rowan of the young lovers walking by arm in arm amidst flowers of every color that were blooming in the field. He described the fine view of a beautiful skyline that could be seen in the distance.

As Olvar described everything he could see outside the tent opening in exquisite detail, Rowan would close his eyes and imagine the picturesque scene described to him.

One warm afternoon, Olvar described a celebration outside.

Although Rowan couldn't hear the music – he could see it in his mind's eye as the fallen warrior by the tent opening portrayed it with descriptive words.

Days and days passed.

One morning, when one of the women came to

bring water, she found the lifeless body of Olvar who had died peacefully in his sleep.

Rowan was saddened as she called some of the camp's men to take his body away.

He had become quite attached to the man who had taught him how to fight and who had protected him when the horseman was upon him.

Being that the bandages across his eyes were off and he was starting to see better, Rowan asked if he could be moved next to the tent opening so he could enjoy the view outside himself.

The woman was happy to make the switch and after making sure he was comfortable, she left him alone.

Slowly and painfully, Rowan propped himself up on one elbow to take his first look at the real world outside in a long time.

He strained to slowly turn to look out the tent opening.

He saw a bush.

Although you could easily get in and out of the tent, there was a bush blocking the view of anything beyond that.

"There's no view," he said.

The woman looked behind her at the bush and then looked back down at him.

"No, I'm sorry," she said. "Maybe when you're able to be moved, we can find a better spot."

"Olvar, the man that was in here with me. Each day when he was sat up, he would look out of the tent opening and describe the view and everything happening outside to me."

He looked outside at the bush again.

"But there's been a bush blocking the view the whole time," he said. "I wonder what could have compelled him to have described such wonderful things outside the tent's opening?"

"He'd been blinded by a sword slash and could not even see the bush," she said. "Perhaps he was just trying to keep your spirits up."

# Chapter 26

It was only a few more days before Rowan was well enough to walk around and leave the hospitality of his caretakers. He'd learned of the battle's results and that the Karlings had been pushed back, but at a great loss to the tribesmen.

They had returned his ax and helm to him.

His helm had been smashed. Most likely from being stepped on by a horse. They'd taken his broken shield and tossed the wood with the rest of them scattered on the battlefield for the funeral pyres. His helmet he could probably hammer back into shape.

He watched the funeral pyre of Olvar. An older man had come and set it ablaze. Rowan watched him as he stood by the pyre watching it burn.  He looked familiar to him, but Rowan wasn't quite sure.  He'd sat off to the distance by himself overlooking all the other funeral pyres. There were many.

Rowan was now at a loss as to what to do or where to go. They said the Karlings would be back with a larger force and perhaps he'd have another chance to win some lands. But for now he was still at a loss.

Some men were going to stay and wait for their chance once again. Others were simply returning to their homelands. That was a possible option for him, but he feared that he'd face much of the same problems that led to him coming out here in the first place.

He heard a few men suggest to others about going to the various tribes and asking to join their people. He also heard others talk of taking their chances and trying to find other lands elsewhere to the south.

There seemed to be seats available on just about every longboat leaving, regardless of which direction it was going.

"Hello Rowan," he heard someone say next him.

Rowan looked up at the man speaking to him and immediately recognized him as the man who'd lit Olvar's funeral pyre.

Getting a closer look at him, Rowan recognized him even more. It was the trader that had taken him from the burning rubble of his home when his

346

parents were killed by raiders. It was the man who took him across the sea and sold him to the blacksmith as a thrall.

"I have been looking for you," he said. "Rowan, son of Bran, son of Ingvald."

"What?"

"I am your mother's uncle."

A mixture of feelings ran through Rowan. Those of hatred for selling him off as a thrall and those of gratitude for rescuing him from the burning ruins. But the feelings that ran the most were those of confusion.

"My mother's uncle?"

"Yes," he said. "I traveled back to the blacksmith in search of you. They told me of what happened and they told me that you might be here helping the tribes defend their lands from the Karlings."

Rowan, confused and still trying to put everything together, said, "you were at the funeral pyre of Olvar."

"That is correct." he said. "It grieves me to see his passing. I came to deliver bad news to him about the death of his son, Sven. But I guess he already knows this because he met him in Valhalla."

"You knew Olvar personally?"

"Yes, but that is not the main reason why I've come," he said. "I have come for you."

"Come for me? I am no thrall to be taken and sold. You sold me once, you will not sell me again.

Rowan grabbed his ax and began to get up to his feet.

"Relax," he said. "I have not come to sell you. You are more than just a thrall or karl, Rowan. You must understand, when I sold you as a thrall that it was to protect you from being discovered. I hid you in the very last place they'd ever look for you."

"Hid me," Rowan said while lowering his ax. "Hid me where?"

"Right in their very own backyard," he said cheerfully.

"I don't understand," Rowan said.

"The Lady of the Woods will not rest until her husband rests," he said. "Come, there is much to tell. It is time to take you home and reclaim your birth right."

*~The End~*

"Just because I can't speak doesn't mean I have
nothing to say!"

**Spread Autism Awareness.**

It no longer just affects a few families here and there.

It now affects us all.

9 781943 066230